'Is the ide... unpalatable t...

'No,' Stephanie answered slowly. ... know if it's a good idea. You have your daughter arriving tomorrow, and I'm no expert, but the last thing she'll need while she's adjusting to a new country is a new woman in her father's life.'

She had a point, and it wasn't one he liked as he knew it was pretty accurate. Still a part of him wanted to know. 'My daughter aside, do you find the prospect of dating me so...bad?'

Stephanie couldn't help but smile at him. 'Not...bad *per se*. I just don't think it's a good idea right now.'

'So where does that leave us? Friends?'

She nodded in agreement, yet the look they shared across the bench was a mutual acknowledgement that they were both fooling themselves.

Dear Reader

Whilst recently visiting the Blue Mountains, I read the local paper and found a snippet where several people at the local hospital had shaved their heads to raise money for cancer. This, naturally, led to the idea for my wonderful and gutsy heroine, Stephanie, shaving her head for such a worthy cause.

Unlike Stephanie, I doubt I'd have the guts to shave my own hair off, let alone colour it bright green! Then again, Stephanie is a very unique woman who is always bubbly and happy. I knew I needed to find the perfect hero for her, and I did. Oliver is simply gorgeous, and I adore the way he has no idea how to deal with his daughter yet loves her so deeply. Stephanie not only helps Oliver to open up but, in turn, Oliver helps Stephanie to do the same.

Coming Home to Katoomba was such a wonderful and heart-warming book to write. I sincerely hope you enjoy it.

With warmest regards,

Lucy Clark

Recent titles by the same author:

UNDERCOVER DOCTOR
DR CUSACK'S SECRET SON
CRISIS AT KATOOMBA HOSPITAL

COMING HOME
TO KATOOMBA

BY
LUCY CLARK

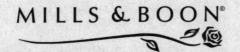

To my darling Dad,
Aren't you glad I never got my head shaved! Thanks for always
loving me, regardless of hairstyle. Psalm 128

*First published in Great Britain 2005
Harlequin Mills & Boon Limited,
Eton House, 18-24 Paradise Road, Richmond, Surrey TW9 1SR*

© Lucy Clark 2005

ISBN 0 263 84335 1

*Set in Times Roman 10½ on 11½ pt.
03-1005-48759*

*Printed and bound in Spain
by Litografia Rosés, S.A., Barcelona*

CHAPTER ONE

STEPHANIE parked her car in the doctors' car park and walked briskly towards the hospital administration building. They'd paged her three times—twice when she'd been having coffee with her good friend Nicolette and once in the car on the drive from Blackheath to Katoomba. She checked her cellphone as she walked and realised she'd forgotten to charge the battery again.

She entered the warm building, glad to be out of the early evening cold, and headed to the CEO's office. Katoomba hospital, about two hours from Sydney, was a mix of old and new wings, with corridors everywhere.

'Hi, Darla,' she said cheerfully to the CEO's assistant. 'Sorry you couldn't get me. Forgot to charge my phone again.'

'Never mind.' Darla held out her hands. 'Give me your coat and bag and cellphone—I'll charge it—and go right in. They're waiting for you.'

Stephanie unwound her scarf and shrugged out of her winter coat. 'They?'

'The new director,' Darla whispered.

'He wasn't due for another five days.' Stephanie's tone was also low, as she handed over the cellphone.

'He's here now.'

'What's his name again?'

'Oliver Bowan.'

'Oliver Bowan,' Stephanie repeated. 'That's right. The man who's taking my job.'

'Your temporary job, and just as a heads-up, he's quite

a dish. I wouldn't mind working alongside him every day.'
Darla sighed dramatically and Stephanie smiled.

'I pictured him as grey, balding with a comb-over.'

Darla laughed out loud and then quickly covered her
mouth. 'Then you're in for a shock. Go.' She angled her
head towards the door behind her which led to the CEO's
office.

Stephanie took a deep breath, briefly knocking on the
door before heading in. 'Sorry it took me so long to get
here, Graham.' She breezed into the room, both men standing at her presence.

'That's fine, Stephanie. I'd like you to meet Oliver
Bowan.'

She turned and looked at her new boss for the first time
and realised Darla was one hundred per cent correct. What
a dish! His dark brown hair was short at the sides with a
hint of grey at the temples, parted at the side with a lock
falling across his forehead. He pushed it back impatiently,
his fingers leaving faint tracks in the thick waves. Definitely
not a comb-over. She smiled to herself and held out her
hand. His skin touched hers the instant their gazes met and
in that brief moment it felt as though the world had stopped
revolving and tilted precariously on its axis.

A warm tingling sensation spread from her fingertips up
her arm before being amplified throughout her entire body.
His eyes were blue—an ice-blue so light and so fresh…
She was mesmerised. He was looking at her with something
like complete astonishment, his jaw slack for a moment
before he recovered.

'I'm pleased to meet you.'

Oh, his deep, rich tone fitted perfectly with the rest of
him. 'Finally.' Stephanie squeezed his hand once more before reluctantly letting go. She saw his stunned gaze sur-
veying her hair and her earrings. 'Not what you were expecting, eh?' She chuckled and so did Graham. 'I guess

most people think green hair and medicine don't usually go together.'

'Stephanie was a brave participant in ''Shave for a Cure'' about two weeks ago,' Graham explained. 'Before that, she had a lovely head of reddish-gold curls.'

'Both the colour and the curls were from a bottle, so it was no great loss.' She shrugged. 'Besides, we raised quite a bit of money so it was worth it.'

'I see,' Oliver replied, even if he wasn't quite sure that he did.

'We weren't expecting you until Saturday,' Stephanie remarked.

'I had a change of plans.'

'Oliver's more than happy to take over straight away,' Graham was saying, and Stephanie reluctantly dragged her gaze away from the man beside her to look at the CEO. 'I presume that's fine with you?'

'Absolutely.'

'I thought as much,' Graham was saying. 'Stephanie's home burned down a few weeks ago, such a tragedy, so she's been under more pressure than usual.'

'I'm sorry to hear that. I hope no one was hurt.'

'My neighbour, Mrs Malincotty, is in the burns unit in Sydney but she's doing OK.'

'Good news, then.' Once more their gazes met and Stephanie couldn't help the involuntary smile that lit her features. It was as though they were having two completely different conversations. One with their eyes and one with their words. The eyes one was much more interesting, she decided. 'It sounds as though you've had an extremely busy time.'

'You can say that again. House burning down on Sunday night, head shaved on Tuesday. That's life, but it could have been a lot worse.'

'I'm glad you have such a positive outlook on life.'

'What other is there to have?' She shrugged again.

'Good philosophy,' Graham added. 'Right. All the paperwork is done. I'll get Darla to process everything so, Stephanie, if you wouldn't mind showing Oliver around and introducing him to the trauma unit staff, that about wraps things up.' Graham stood and held out his hand to Oliver. 'Welcome to the Blue Mountains and Katoomba hospital,' he said officially.

Stephanie got to her feet as the two men shook hands. 'Let's go.' She opened the door and waited, expecting Oliver to follow her. He did, but first he picked up a large suitcase which she hadn't noticed in the corner of the room. 'You've *just* arrived?'

He glanced down at the suitcase, then back to her. 'Obviously.' There was a twinkle behind his eyes, even though he wasn't smiling.

'Are you mocking me?'

'Yes.'

'Oh. OK.' She smiled at the CEO. 'Thanks, Graham.' She headed out to Darla and picked up her cellphone, bag, coat and scarf. 'You were right,' she whispered to the assistant. 'Very dishy.' The two women smiled before Oliver came out of the office, suitcase trailing like a puppy behind him.

'Not going to be macho and carry it?' Stephanie couldn't resist teasing.

'I'd rather conserve my energy for dealing with my insubordinate staff.'

It was Stephanie's turn to stare, slack-jawed for a split second before she laughed, Darla and Graham joining in.

'All right, then, Dr Bowan. Let's go meet the troops.' They left the CEO's office and headed along an internal corridor so they didn't have to go back outside into the cold. 'I think you'll find the rest of the staff quite placid in comparison to me. Well...' Stephanie looked him up and down, taking in the pin-striped suit '…some of the nurses might be a little, shall we say, flirtatious but I'm not going to tell you which ones. That, you'll just have to find out for yourself.'

'So no one else has a brightly coloured head?'

'Nope. I'm unique.'

'Something I've already come to realise.' He was look-ing again at her ears and she subconsciously lifted a hand to one ear. Now that her hair was so much shorter, the four sets of earrings she wore were definitely more prominent.

'Hey—you can directly blame my brother for these. He keeps buying me the most beautiful earrings and I want to wear them all at once.'

'Ever thought of changing them daily?'

'I do.' Stephanie smiled and turned a corner before head-ing to the lifts and punching the button. 'We can stow your case in my office—uh, well your office now—and then go meet the staff that are here.'

'Thank you, Dr Brooks.'

'I hope you're not going to continue with that.'

'Pardon?'

'Dr Brooks.'

'No, I'm Dr Bowan.'

Stephanie smiled. 'You know what I mean. Call me Stephanie or Steph, whichever takes your fancy.' The lift arrived and she went in, holding the door for him and his suitcase. 'Just the one bag? Surely, as this is a permanent job for you here in the Blue Mountains, you'll have more than one bag.' She punched the button for two floors below and the old lift doors slowly began to shut.

'This is all, for now.'

'Fair enough. Where are you staying?'

'In a house somewhere. My previous secretary organised temporary accommodation until I have time to look around for a more permanent residence.' He patted his suit jacket pocket. 'It's all written down and the estate agent said they'd leave the key in the letterbox, which I thought was odd.'

'Odd?'

'Leaving the key to a house in a letterbox isn't exactly high security.'

The doors opened and she headed out, looking over her shoulder at him. 'Where have you come from?'

Oliver raised an eyebrow. 'Do you really need a talk on the birds and the bees, *Stephanie*?'

She gave him a bored look. 'Hardly, *Oliver*. It's just if you've come here from a big, bustling city, then a key in the letterbox would seem odd to you.'

He followed her along yet another winding corridor. 'This place is a rabbit warren.'

'You'll get used to it. So? Are you going to answer the question?'

'Seattle.'

'Really?'

'You seem surprised.'

'You don't sound American.'

'I'm Australian. My ex-wife is American.'

'Ah. Currently single, then?' She made sure the question came out casually but she'd already noted the lack of wedding ring, even though it was commonplace for a lot of married doctors not to wear rings.

'Planning to ask me out?' he countered.

Stephanie stopped and looked at him in stunned confusion. Was it possible this man was as direct as her *and* possessed the same sense of humour? Realising he was waiting for an answer, as well as enjoying having knocked her off balance, she tried for an air of nonchalance, tossing her head and continuing their trek through the corridors. 'Play your cards right and there's a definite possibility.'

To her further astonishment and delight, she heard him

chuckle. 'In that case, I am definitely unattached. And you?'

'Here we are,' she said, ignoring his question and unlocking a door. 'Your new office.' She walked in and switched on the light, putting her coat, bag and scarf on a chair. 'Sorry it's a bit messy. If I'd known you were coming—'

'You'd have baked a cake?' he interrupted, as he went further into the room and placed his suitcase against the wall out of the way.

'Well, maybe.' She went around the desk and quickly gathered pieces of paper into neater piles.

'Leave it. I'll have to sort through it all anyway.'

'We should probably go through it together in case you have any questions,' she added. 'First, though, let's get the introductions over.' She waited for him to exit the room, locking the door behind her. 'I presume Darla's organising keys and passes for you?'

'Should be ready tomorrow.'

'Now, let me think who's on tonight. Sophie's here— she's an excellent triage nurse. Jade—she has her head screwed on right and I think Lauren's on, too. Hmm... Lauren.' Stephanie frowned, thinking of the perky brunette nurse who would definitely be employing her expert flirting skills with the new trauma unit boss.

'What about Lauren?'

Stephanie smiled and pretended to lock her lips and throw away the key.

'Ah. One of the ones I should watch out for, eh? Noted.'

'Who knows? She might be your type.'

'Know me that well, Dr Brooks?'

'No. That's why I said *might*, Dr Bowan.' Stephanie swiped her card through a lock and pushed open the door. 'Here we are.' She'd been conscious of Oliver walking next to her the entire way from Graham's office to her own but now, entering the A and E department where quite a few staff members momentarily stopped to watch them walk towards the nurses' station, Stephanie was totally aware of the man beside her.

There was a mild, spicy scent around him and she wondered how much travelling he'd done that day. Why had he come to the hospital immediately he'd arrived in the district? Eager to do his work? Perhaps using it as a test to see how both the hospital and his staff coped with an unexpected arrival?

She wouldn't put it past him and realised the entire time she'd spent in his company had probably been her own test. She groaned quietly and shook her head. She should have been more professional instead of teasing him but... Stephanie shrugged, knowing there was nothing she could do about it now even if she wanted to. Besides, she was who she was and nothing was going to change that.

'Sophie.' Stephanie indicated the nurse at the desk. 'Meet Oliver Bowan, the new trauma unit director.'

Sophie held out her hand, smiling a welcome. 'Good to have you here.' She picked up a file. 'Are you officially on duty?'

'Need help?' he asked briskly, his face serious.

Sophie smiled. 'We're doing just fine tonight. Ah, here are two of my best nurses. Jade and Lauren.' As the two nurses headed across to the desk, Stephanie watched as Lauren, already holding Oliver's gaze, pulled her shoulders back, effectively thrusting out her chest. Sophie introduced them and Lauren encompassed his hand with both of hers, almost stroking his hand as he took a step back.

'Well, isn't this just wonderful?' Lauren crooned, giving Oliver her winning smile. 'With you and Stephen around, we have eye candy galore. Oh, no offence, Steph,' she added quickly. 'Can't blame a girl for looking.'

Stephanie smiled benignly. She didn't care whether or

not Lauren looked at her twin brother because she knew
Stephen was more than capable of holding his own.
Besides, she also knew Stephen was very interested in her
friend Nicolette. He was about to open his own general
practice and Nicolette was going to help him. It wouldn't
be long before both her brother and friend stopped fighting
the natural attraction that existed between them.

Sophie and Jade headed off to see to their patients while
Lauren worked hard to engage Oliver in conversation. He
smiled nicely at the pretty nurse and Stephanie rolled her
eyes and looked away. It appeared Oliver Bowan was going
to have every female within a heartbeat falling for him. She
couldn't stand that kind of man and where she'd felt a spark
with him earlier, it was definitely starting to fizzle out now.

'So, who's this Stephen fellow?' Oliver asked Lauren.

'He's one of the doctors here. He saved Stephanie from
a burning house and it was all very dramatic and heroic,'
Lauren gushed, and then sighed romantically. 'All girls
love that knight-in-shining-armour thing, don't we, Steph?'

'Mmm.' Stephanie grimaced, trying not to look at the
two of them together. When the phone beside her rang, she
snatched it up, glad to have something to do. 'A and E, Dr
Brooks.'

'Stephanie, it's Nicolette. There's been an accident on
the overpass at Medlow Bath. I've called it in but wanted
the hospital to know Stephen and I are on the scene. We're
going to need back-up, and soon.'

'What's the situation?' Stephanie reached for a pen and
piece of paper.

'A coal truck hit a tourist bus, pushing the bus over the
overpass wall. We saw it all. It happened right in front of
us.'

'Oh, my goodness. Is Stephen all right? Are you?'

'We're fine. There was a loud noise but I'm not sure
what it was. Kind of like a huge cracking sound, which

rocked the area. Stephen's just gone to look. I'll call with more info as I get it. Just a second, Steph.'

Stephanie waited impatiently.

'Stephanie?' Oliver asked. 'What's going on?'

She looked at him, amazed he'd been able to drag himself away from Lauren's sparkling repartee. 'Accident in Medlow Bath. Just getting details now.' Nicolette came back on the line.

'Stephen said the train was just coming into the station when the bus went over. The train hit the coach and pushed it along the tracks into the station. I've got to go. Stephen and I both have our phones. Give me a call when you're close.'

'We're on our way.' Stephanie put the phone down and continued writing notes.

'Stephanie?' Oliver was waiting impatiently and she held up one finger for him to wait.

'Just let me get this down.' She finished writing and then stood. 'Lauren, get the trauma unit retrieval team together in the tearoom, stat. We need to move on this quickly.' The nurses headed off and Stephanie went to move as well, but Oliver barred her way.

'Aren't you forgetting something?' His tone was brisk and the way he looked at her was with mild disdain. What was his problem? First he was funny, then he was flirty with Lauren and now he was brisk.

'And that would be?'

'I'm in charge of this unit now.' His words were enough to make her see red.

'Oh, and I suppose you know our procedures?'

'I know what I intend to change.'

'You can do that tomorrow. Right now, we need to get organised. Do you even know where Medlow Bath is?'

'As a matter of fact, I do as I've studied a map of the area. I don't, however, know the way to the tearoom. If you'd be so kind as to lead the way…' Oliver trailed off, stepping back to let her pass.

'Thank you.' The words were clipped and as she strode off, he kept pace beside her.

'You're right, though. We'll start on implementing new procedures tomorrow. For tonight, introduce me to the staff, give the briefing and I'll take it from there. Although I don't know your procedures, I am highly qualified in trauma medicine. Is your Stephen?'

'Stephen?'

'I presume he's on the scene?'

'Yes.'

'I'm merely asking if he's trained enough to handle this situation.'

Stephanie was offended for both her brother and her friend. 'He and Nicolette have both worked in war zones. I'd say they're more than qualified to handle emergency trauma.'

'Good.' His tone was brisk.

Who was this man? She turned the corner and walked into the tearoom. Where was the man who'd accompanied her from the admin building? Oliver Bowan was like a chameleon and she now wasn't so sure she liked him at all. 'First impressions can be deceptive,' she mumbled to herself.

'Pardon?'

'Nothing.' Staff were starting to arrive and once the team was assembled, Stephanie introduced Oliver and gave the debrief before stepping aside. True to his word, he started to give out jobs to staff members and within a few minutes they were all heading off to get changed into the bright orange retrieval suits, which were made with many different ent pockets, perfect for holding the equipment they needed. People gathered together what they thought they'd need and headed out to the waiting ambulances.

Oliver climbed into one of the transport vehicles, noticing that Stephanie chose a different one to go in. She was angry with him. Although he'd known her for less than an hour, he knew she was angry. What he couldn't figure out was, why? He'd been surprised at how easily they'd jumped right into conversation from the instant they'd met. It was as though they were old friends who hadn't seen each other for years and had just picked up where they'd left off.

He'd really enjoyed their friendly banter and for a brief moment he'd decided he wouldn't mind getting to know her better. When Lauren had apologised to Stephanie for ogling Stephen—whoever he was—Oliver had been surprised. Who was this Stephen and why should Lauren have apologised? He then realised Stephanie hadn't answered his question about her own relationship status. Was she involved with him? She'd certainly jumped to Stephen's defence when he'd questioned the other doctor's ability to cope with a large accident scene. If this Stephen bloke had worked in a war zone, he definitely knew how to handle trauma…but, then, so did he himself.

This was his show now. Oliver breathed deeply at the thought, glad no one had questioned him regarding the briefing. Katoomba hospital Administration was relying on him to take the A and E and trauma unit and shape it into an efficient team. This was his unit and he would run it his way, making his own decisions, and no wacky, green-spiky-haired, crazy doctor was going to deter him from his job.

The fact he found her extremely sexy had nothing to do with it. Nothing at all!

CHAPTER TWO

WHEN they finally arrived at the scene, the police making a path for the emergency vehicles, Oliver started issuing orders left, right and centre.

'I want at least two paramedics on the station platform to do triage.' He turned to a police officer. 'We're going to need a temporary base. Is there anywhere close that is large enough to be our casualty base? Once patients are ready to be moved, they can go there until the ambulances are available to either take them to Katoomba or, if they need to be transferred to Sydney, we can get that transportation organised.'

'There's the health resort just down there.' The police officer pointed to a large building, dating from around the 1850s, which had been renovated to retain its old-world glory and charm.

'Perfect. Get someone onto it.'

Stephanie walked up to Oliver. 'I called Nic on the way here and she said to start with the bus. She and Stephen are in the train.'

'Right.' Oliver nodded.

'Police rescue's here,' someone else told him.

Oliver nodded and again set about giving people jobs. She had to admire the way he was handling the situation. For the new boy on the block, he certainly did know his stuff.

Stephanie headed towards the bus, shocked at what she saw. It was lying on its side, jammed on the tracks between the station platforms. Some of the passengers had managed

17

to push open the back emergency window and, with assistance, were starting to climb out.

'Wait!' both Oliver and Stephanie called. Oliver turned and barked an order over his shoulder. One of the police rescue officers came over. 'Take over getting these people safely out. The last thing we need is people jumping from the bus and breaking their legs.'

'I'm on it,' the police officer told him.

Oliver then stopped a paramedic walking by. 'Everyone must be seen, no matter how insignificant their injuries might seem. I want notes on every single person.'

'Will do.'

Oliver came to Stephanie's side. 'With the passengers being evacuated through the back window, it'll be best if we can get in through the front door. That way, we don't hinder the evacuation procedure.' He paused thoughtfully. 'We're going to need abseiling ropes just to get inside.'

She nodded. 'We'll have to be harnessed.' She sucked in a breath and looked around her, a worried frown on her face.

'Something wrong?'

'Just feeling a little…' She shrugged. 'I don't know, a little claustrophobic.'

'That's not what I want to hear just before I send you into a tourist bus crowded with people.'

Stephanie shook her head and reached for her phone. 'I'll be fine.'

'Who are you calling?' he asked.

'Nic.'

'The other doctor with Stephen?'

'Yes.'

'Good. Let her know what's happening up here.'

Stephanie nodded. 'See that guy over there?' She pointed up to the platform as she pressed a few buttons on her phone. 'That's David, head of police rescue. You can get harnesses and other equipment from him.' She paused, listening to the phone ring then said, 'Nic? Oliver wanted me to let you know the paramedics have taken over the triage on the station platform and the health resort down the road has agreed to act as a base for cases until we can get reinforcements here from Springwood. Is Stephen all right?' There was a warning tone in Stephanie's voice.

Oliver couldn't be bothered listening. It was obvious Stephanie and her Stephen were so close she couldn't let him out of her sight. Hadn't she just checked on the man not that long ago? Oliver headed off towards David, pushing thoughts of Stephanie Brooks from his mind. He was there to work and he needed to get things moving.

A minute later, Stephanie joined him and listened as David gave them both instructions. 'I know Stephanie's done this quite a few times before. I take it you're the same?' he asked Oliver.

'Yes.' They both climbed into their harnesses and walked with David over to where they would enter the bus.

'Right. Billy and Krystal need a few more minutes to finish setting up the Larkin frame. Let's run through things. We need to get hooked up to the winch ropes one at a time. I'll go first, then Steph, then you, Oliver. The winch ropes will support you as you climb up the bus and once we're ready to go inside, it'll lower you down.'

Oliver looked at the Larkin frame—a large structure with a winch on it. 'That'll support us?'

'Absolutely, mate. It's also the best way for us to get in and out—for now. So, once we're at the top of the bus, we'll open the doors and get you to your patients. Once you're in the bus, undo the winch rope and you'll be able to move about freely and attend the injured. Questions?' Both Stephanie and Oliver shook their heads. 'All righty, then. Let's get to work.'

She'd known the police rescue officer for quite some

time and although they'd gone out a few times, there was no spark and she was glad they'd been able to remain friends. She knew people thought she had an abundance of confidence and in her professional life she did, but, personally, getting close to a man was something she'd struggled with. She could flirt, she could laugh and enjoy herself, but letting someone inside her barriers was not something she found easy to do.

'I hear you've finally managed to coax Stephen to the area,' David said conversationally as he hooked his D-clamp to the winch rope.

'Yes.' Stephanie grinned and then sighed dramatically. 'And about time, too. I thought I might turn grey if he stayed in that war zone any longer.'

David pointed to her head. 'Instead, you turned green, eh? Let's get a hard hat with a light on it in case those spikes cause any more damage.'

'Oh, you're funny. Actually, Stephen's in the front carriage of the train, tending to a boy with a possible rupture to his femoral artery. I've just organised equipment to be sent to him and Nic.'

'That's good. Coax him to the Blue Mountains and send him to work.'

Stephanie's smile broadened. 'Wouldn't have it any other way.'

'Can we get this show on the road?' Oliver barked, sick and tired of hearing about Stephen. It was now obvious that Stephanie was involved with the man but it meant nothing to him. She obviously hadn't meant anything by her earlier flirting and he'd been a fool to read anything into it. If the woman was taken then so be it. He wasn't looking for any commitments anyway. With his daughter due to arrive in a few days, he had enough to worry about.

'Certainly.' Stephanie's tone was brisk.

'What about your claustrophobia?' Oliver asked.

'There's no point going through all this if you're going to be useless once you're inside.'

'Stephanie doesn't have claustrophobia,' David stated, calling for helmets on his walkie-talkie.

'I felt a little…closed in before,' she explained to David. 'Stephen was jammed. I felt it.'

David laughed.

Oliver rolled his eyes.

'I'm fine now,' she insisted.

'Good,' Oliver snapped. 'Now, can we leave Stephen in the train and concentrate on the bus, *please*?'

Again Stephanie frowned. 'Of course.' They both received their helmets and after Billy and Krystal had finished with the Larkin frame, they watched David scale the bus with minimal effort.

'Winch rope ready for Stephanie.' David's voice came through Billy's radio.

'Ready, Steph?' Billy asked.

'As I'll ever be.' She waited until the winch rope was secure before starting her climb. She tried hard to follow the foot- and hand-holds David had used, but realised she was a little shorter than him so figured out her own.

'You made it look so easy,' she grumbled when she was almost at the top.

'Lie flat,' David told her as she came over the lip. He unhooked her rope and radioed down to Billy. Stephanie lay flat, as she was told, trying to see in through the tinted bus windows to the patients inside while they waited for Oliver. She glanced at her colleague, only to see him climb up as easily as David had.

'Men,' she muttered.

'Pardon?' Oliver glared at her.

'Nothing,' she said sweetly, pasting on a smile.

David found the emergency release for the door but it didn't work. 'Looks as though we'll have to do this the old-fashioned way.' A moment later, he'd pried open the doors and locked them in place. He hooked himself up to the winch rope and radioed to Billy and Krystal to start the winch. He went down first, leaving Stephanie and Oliver at the top.

'Mentally running through scenarios?' she asked Oliver, who looked so serious he was almost frightening.

'Yes. Goodness knows what we're going to find.'

'I'm in,' David called. 'Hook your D-clamp to the winch rope and come on down, Steph.'

'OK. I'm ready,' she said, and once more he radioed for the winch to go.

She slowly descended, flicking on her helmet lamp. Outside, the strong stench of spilt fuel had dominated the air, with emergency crews working hard to ensure nothing exploded. Inside the bus, another smell dominated. As she made her way vertically into the horizontal bus, death seemed to surround her. She'd never been able to find the words to describe the smell and sometimes she couldn't actually smell anything, but it was here now and she schooled her features, pulling her professional mask into place.

As well as the lights on their helmets, David was rigging up a temporary source of light which would help them see the devastation before them. Once she was down, it was Oliver's turn. Stephanie wasn't quite sure where to start but pulled out a pair of gloves from her retrieval suit. During her ambulance ride, she'd packed the pockets with several items such as gloves, bandages and a penlight torch.

'Check the driver,' Oliver instructed, and Stephanie carefully made her way over to her first patient.

'Can you hear me?' she called to the driver. He was still in his seat, his head hanging forward, blood trickling down the side of his face and around his ear. She placed her hand on his shoulder and squeezed firmly. 'Hello?'

He moaned.

'Help is here. Can you talk?' As she spoke, a medical kit was lowered through the forced-open doorway. 'My name is Stephanie. What's yours?'

'Earl.'

'Hey, Earl. We'll get you out of here soon.'

'The passengers.'

'We have people taking care of them. I'm just going to check you over to see what the damage is. Can you move your legs? Wiggle your toes?'

'Yes.'

'Good. We'll get you stabilised and then get you out of here.' She checked his pulse and didn't like the feel of it. She reached into the medical kit and unfolded the cervical collar. 'Earl, let's lean your head back a little so I can put this collar on. Then I'll take a good look at you.' She carefully fitted the collar, noting the amount of blood on his face. He had several lacerations that would require suturing. 'How are you doing, Earl?'

He murmured something incoherent but at least he was responding to her. She applied gauze pads to his lacerations and then bandaged his head, keeping them in place and applying the necessary pressure to control the flow of blood. Thankfully, the medical kit she'd been passed was set up for emergencies just like this and contained a bag of saline.

'How are you doing, Steph?' Oliver called.

'Five more minutes and I'm all yours.'

'Now, there's an offer you can't refuse,' David joked from down the back of the bus.

'You know what I mean,' she retorted. She inserted the cannula into Earl's arm and hooked the bag of saline over the edge of the front window visor. 'Earl? Earl, can you hear me?'

Again, incoherent mumbling. She reached for the medical torch and checked his pupils. Both were reacting to light but one was slightly larger than the other. 'David, can we get Earl out and airlifted to Sydney…?'

'I'll get that organised for you,' David called, and radioed out to his staff.

One of the paramedics was just coming in through the door and Stephanie grabbed him and directed him to monitor Earl while she went to help Oliver.

'What have we got?'

Oliver turned, his face so close to hers she gasped. Even after the day he'd had, travelling and now this, she could still smell his underlying spicy scent. His breath was warm on her cheek as he spoke softly. 'Two people are dead but the woman trapped between them is alive. She's regained consciousness once and told me her name is Michelle. She doesn't know the people on either side of her are dead. It's going to take quite some time to cut them out as the seats have sandwiched them together. David's getting equipment organised now.'

Stephanie slowly exhaled and shook her head. 'Michelle's injuries?'

'She was having trouble breathing so I've requested oxygen. Hopefully, it'll be here soon.'

'Her airway's not blocked?'

'No. I think the problem is her chest but it's a little hard to get to it. Basically, we can give her oxygen and something for the pain, but until she's free there's not much we can do.'

'Obs?'

'Have you got a portable sphygmo in your kit?'

Stephanie checked and came up trumps, pulling it out and wrapping the cuff around Michelle's free arm. 'Michelle?' Stephanie called. 'My name is Stephanie and I'm just going to check your blood pressure.'

A groan came from the woman. 'Hang in there,

Michelle,' Oliver said as he checked her pupils again, letting her know what he was doing. 'I'm going to give you something for the pain. Do you know if you're allergic to anything?'

'Pethidine,' Michelle murmured.

'OK. Thanks.' Oliver checked through the medical kit.

'BP is ninety over forty.'

'Let's get a bag of saline up and going.'

'Do you have one in your kit?' Stephanie asked. 'I used mine for the bus driver.'

'Yes. Here's one.' He pulled out the packets she needed and Stephanie opened them, pulling out the cannula and getting everything hooked together. 'Michelle?' Oliver called again, but this time received no reply. 'Michelle?' he called a little louder. 'Can you hear me, Michelle? We're going to put a drip in your hand and then we'll give you some morphine.'

Oliver helped Stephanie, hooking the saline bag onto the bus's overhead handrail. Once that was done, he drew up an injection of morphine and administered it, flushing it through. David came to check on them. 'How much longer?' Oliver asked.

'We're getting the equipment winched in now. Billy's overseeing that. We have two more patients down the back who need your attention. Is she stable?' He pointed to Michelle.

'As stable as we can get her. Her name is Michelle,' Stephanie said.

'Does she have any idea…?' David spoke softly and pointed to the people on either side of her.

'No.'

'Going to tell her?'

'Not just yet. Her body has enough to deal with,' Oliver replied. 'The morphine should help her relax a little so she'll be drowsy.'

'Do her obs in two more minutes,' Stephanie suggested, as she gathered up her medical kit. Oliver did the same. 'The two down in the corner?' she asked, pointing.

'Yes.' A call came over David's radio, informing him they were bringing in a stretcher to winch Earl out. The police rescue staff had popped out the front windscreen to enable them to get stretchers in and out more easily.

'Good. Make sure they do his obs before they move him and keep a close watch on his pupils,' Stephanie demanded.

'Will do,' David said, and they left him to organise his staff as well as monitor Michelle.

Stephanie and Oliver clambered their way over seats and debris towards the two people at the back.

'You take one, I'll take the other,' Oliver said from behind her.

'Acknowledged.' Stephanie finally reached her patient. 'Hi, I'm Stephanie.'

'Troy,' the man said, a grimace on his face.

'Where does it hurt?'

'My left leg. I can't move it.'

Stephanie carefully shifted down. 'Foot? Ankle? Thigh? Whereabouts is the most pain?'

'Around my knee.'

Stephanie pulled on a fresh pair of gloves and tentatively touched the area. Troy winced. 'Really bad, eh? Sorry. If you can bear with me for a bit longer, I'll try not to hurt you too much.' She lifted the lower part of his leg and gently extended it. 'How much pain?'

Troy was gritting his teeth and moaning but didn't answer her.

'Quite a bit. Right. Do you play any sport?'

'Rugby.'

'Have you ever injured your knee before?' As she spoke she opened her medical kit and pulled out the sphygmomanometer and shifted up to wind the cuff around Troy's arm.

'About two months ago.'

'Have any work done on it?'

'Just physio.'

'You may need some work done now. Nothing feels broken but we'll get you stabilised and off to the hospital for X-rays and a consultation with one of our orthopaedic surgeons.'

'What do you think it is?'

'At a guess I'd say your medial ligament's been torn. The fact that you damaged your knee not so long ago means the ligament was weakening. You would have put a lot of stress on your legs, trying to stop yourself from falling, when the crash happened.' She listened for a second before pulling the stethoscope from her ears. 'Blood pressure's good, considering the trauma you've been through. Are you allergic to anything?'

'No.'

'OK. I'm going to give you something for the pain, put a couple of bandages around your knee and then hopefully we can get you out.'

'Has…?' Troy stopped and cleared his throat. 'Has anyone died?' He asked the question quietly and Stephanie merely nodded. 'I think I'm gonna be sick.'

'No. You'll be fine.' Stephanie administered the injection. 'This will help. Just close your eyes and concentrate on your breathing. Tell me what the physio said about your knee.'

She kept Troy talking as she stabilised his knee, splinting it with his other leg and ending with a figure of eight bandage around his feet. 'There you go. How are you feeling now?'

'More relaxed.'

'Good. Close your eyes and we'll get you out of here as

soon as we can.' Stephanie moved to look up the bus and winced as the cutting equipment David and his team were using was switched on and a squealing sound filled the air. She checked Troy, who'd opened his eyes wide.

'It's all right,' she soothed him. 'They need to cut through some of the seats to get some of the passengers out. Try and block it out, Troy.' She put her hand on his shoulder and squeezed reassuringly.

She looked around for Oliver and found him at the front, looking up, waiting for something to come down on the winch. When the cutting equipment stopped, she headed towards him and then realised he was carrying a small oxygen cylinder with a non-rebreather mask. David and Billy waited while Oliver performed obs on Michelle and fitted the mask over her nose and mouth, adjusting the cylinder to give her the required dose.

'How's she doing?' Stephanie called. David was pulling hard on the metal they'd just cut through, bending it back.

'Same,' Oliver replied.

'OK,' David said. 'Stand back, we're ready to go again.' A second later, the cutting machine started up again, its high-pitched squeal filling the air once more. Stephanie crawled back and checked on Troy and Oliver's patient. Krystal appeared at the rear emergency-escape window.

'Hey, Steph. Have you got someone else ready to come out?'

'Two here. Both need stretchers.'

'It'll be easier getting them out this exit rather than taking them to the front. I'll get it organised.'

'Thanks.'

Krystal disappeared and at the same time the cutter stopped its whining. The instant it did, Stephanie's phone rang. She glanced down the bus and, amazingly, through all the dust and debris, she could still make out Oliver's scowl.

She answered the call, knowing it was Stephen. 'Hi. Your patient stable?' she asked. She was conscious of her new boss's disapproval but she couldn't figure out why he felt that way.

'For now. Where do you need us?'

'Oliver and I are in the bus. The driver has been taken out and is hopefully being airlifted to Sydney as we speak. Three people are dead and another is trapped—between two of the deceased. She's stable for now and the emergency crews are in the process of cutting her out.' She heard him telling Nicolette the information.

'Head to the health resort?' he asked.

'Yes. I'll catch up with you soon.'

When she disconnected the call she found Oliver had climbed over the seats to check on his patient. He glared at her. 'What?'

'Got your life organised now?' he growled.

'What are you talking about? I'm just getting an update from staff.'

'You mean from Stephen. You are way too preoccupied with that man if you want my opinion.'

Stephanie bristled but spoke quietly. 'Well, I don't want your opinion and Stephen is nothing to do with you. I don't know what your problem is.'

'My problem, as you call it, is that my most senior member of staff isn't concentrating on her job.'

'How dare you?' She made sure her tone was low, not wanting everyone to know they were arguing. 'There's nothing either of us can do right at this moment until the crews have finished removing those seats.'

'I'm not talking about physically but mentally.'

'Are you saying my work isn't up to scratch?'

Oliver frowned. That wasn't what he was saying at all. No, he was annoyed with the way Stephanie was so concerned for her boyfriend. He knew all about suffocating relationships—his ex-wife had been highly demanding. Now she took great pleasure in changing her mind over and over just to bug him. Would he ever be free of the clinging woman? Not while she had custody of their daughter, came the answer. On that score, he was still prepared to fight her tooth and nail to get custody of Kasey.

'Well?' Stephanie demanded when she didn't receive a reply. 'Because if you have a problem with my work performance then I'd prefer you to say it outright. How else am I supposed to adapt and improve, if not with guidance from my peers?'

Oliver swallowed and raked a hand through his hair. Once more he'd managed to annoy her and she had every right to be peeved with him. He shouldn't have jumped down her throat, or tarred her with the same brush as his ex-wife. For all he knew, her Stephen liked being suffocated. Either way, it was nothing to him. *She* was nothing to him except a colleague. 'I'm sorry.' He met her gaze. 'I spoke out of turn. From what I've seen, you're an excellent doctor, Stephanie.'

His soft tone, the slight spark of appreciation behind his eyes gave her a brief glimpse of the man she'd met earlier that evening. It was nice to find he was still lurking beneath the surface. Stephanie was usually pretty good at reading people and for a while there she'd thought she'd read Oliver incorrectly. Now her initial impression returned.

'Thank you.' Her words were a whisper and she sighed with relief. Their gazes held and a small, shy smile touched her lips. Neither of them moved for a moment and it was as though they had been transported to a world that was just their own.

Feeling an increase in her own self-awareness, she reluctantly lowered her gaze, the smile slowly sliding from her lips as she realised that Oliver's opinion of her really mattered to her. She was glad it was favourable but her

stomach began to churn with nervous anticipation. The only
other man's opinion she valued was her brother's.

Why was it suddenly so imperative that she continue to
create such a positive one with Oliver?

That thought scared her more than anything. She glanced
back at him and the churning in her stomach increased. His
gaze was so intense and this time she was powerless to
look away.

CHAPTER THREE

'OK, FOLKS.' David's words intruded into the haze that surrounded them and Stephanie immediately broke her gaze in case she got caught staring into her new boss's gorgeous blue eyes. 'We're ready for you now.'

Back to reality with a thud, she listened to David's briefing.

'The seats have been cut away and Michelle's unconscious again so let's get her out.'

'What's the status on a stretcher for Michelle?' Oliver asked.

'Billy, check with Krystal what's happening,' David ordered. 'All we need to do is pull on each of the seats we've cut and we'll get the leverage we need.'

'We'll need all hands on deck. Stephanie and I need to be able to get to Michelle the instant she's free.'

'Billy?' David asked impatiently.

'Krystal's got the stretcher on the winch and is ready to bring it in through the front windscreen. She's also organising for the two patients down the back to be taken out through the rear window.'

'Good. Once that stretcher's here, we'll begin.'

'How do you want to play this?' Stephanie asked Oliver.

'I think the easiest way is to get the stretcher as close as possible, you support her shoulders, I'll take her legs and we'll transfer her straight to the stretcher.'

'She's really jammed in there. What about internal fractures?'

'Nothing we can do until she's on that stretcher.'

'Good. I concur.'

'Were you just testing me?'

'No. Just making sure we were on the same page. I'll give her a quick check while we're waiting.' Stephanie did what observations she could and soon the stretcher was being hauled down as close to Michelle as possible.

'Stephanie and I will lift her out but we'll need help manoeuvring her so as soon as you're able, lend a hand.' Oliver nodded to both Billy and David. 'Everyone ready?'

'Yes,' they all answered.

'On three. One…two…three.' David and Billy each pulled back as hard as they could on the seats. With this, the top body was released and they were able to remove it.

Stephanie literally muscled her way in and hooked her arms under Michelle's armpits while Oliver used a similar tactic and managed to get a firm hold on Michelle's legs. 'Shift,' he yelled, and Stephanie called on all her inner strength.

Michelle was the one they could help. Those were the words which kept echoing around her head as they finally shifted her free from her position. It was slow, hard work, especially when the entire area wasn't stable. Being able to do this on a flat floor would have been hard enough, but with the bus tipped on its side it was almost impossible…*almost*. Billy came around, ducking beneath them, and was able to help by supporting Michelle from underneath as they carried her to the waiting stretcher. David had unhooked the saline bag and was holding it up.

'Strap her in and let's go.' Oliver's tone was brisk and Stephanie glanced at him. The strain on his face matched hers but at least they'd been able to get Michelle out. Billy crawled through the wreckage, positioning himself at the foot of the stretcher as Oliver listened to Michelle's chest. 'Possible pneumothorax.'

'Michelle?' Stephanie called, and received a mild groan. 'We're getting you out. Hang in there.' She glanced up at David. 'Is there an ambulance standing by?'

'There will be,' he said, and called it in on his radio.

Eventually they had the stretcher ready to hook up to the winch and Krystal was ready to get the show on the road. Once Michelle was on her way down, Oliver turned to David. 'I'll climb out the front windscreen. I need to be there once she's down.'

David nodded and soon Oliver was disappearing through the open windscreen. He turned to Stephanie. 'You're next. We can take it from here.'

Stephanie glanced at Troy and the other patient down at the end but a member of the police rescue staff was there, monitoring both patients. She looked at David and then back at the two that had held Michelle captive.

'You're turning as green as your hair, Steph. Control your thoughts and get out of here. We can take it and you're no help to those two.'

'OK.' She allowed David and Billy to help her over the edge of the windscreen and soon she was out, breathing in the cool, evening air. Even the faint smell of fuel wasn't as bad as the stench in the bus. It was good to feel terra firma beneath her feet again and Stephanie rushed over to Oliver who was once more listening closely to Michelle's chest.

'Status?'

'Fractured ribs with a penetrating chest wound.' Michelle's top had been cut away and now that she was flat, they could see the blood coming from the right side of her chest. 'Her lung may collapse.' He pulled off his stethoscope as he spoke and reached for the first-aid kit.

Stephanie was there first, ripping a square gauze pad from its wrapper. She handed Oliver the wrapper and pulled out some tape. She broke off three pieces, handing them to Oliver. He stuck the plastic gauze wrapper over the wound, sealing in three sides but leaving the fourth open to allow fluid and air to escape. If they could avoid air getting into the space between the two layers of the pleura, her lung might not collapse.

'Get me an oximeter so we can check her oxygen levels.'

Stephanie found one and hooked it onto Michelle's finger. A moment later, she had her reading. 'Ninety per cent.'

'Good. Michelle? It's Oliver. We're getting ready to transfer you to hospital.' He checked her pupils and smiled when Michelle tried to pull away from his touch. 'Good. You're out of the bus, Michelle, and the ambulance is waiting to take you to hospital.'

Oliver turned and spoke to the paramedic. 'We're needed here so you take her. Call ahead because I want not only a general surgeon waiting for her but an orthopaedic surgeon as well. Once she's stabilised, get her off to Sydney. Priority one.'

'Yes, Doctor.'

Once Michelle was in the ambulance and being taken to hospital, Oliver turned and looked at Stephanie. 'Are you all right?'

She nodded.

Oliver placed both hands on her shoulders. 'Stephanie, I mean it. That wasn't the usual run-of-the-mill rescue.'

'I know. I'll process. I'll filter.' She shrugged. 'Stephen will help me through it. He always does.' At the mention of Stephen's name, Oliver dropped his hands. 'How about you?'

'Just like you, I'll be fine.' He stalked off, leaving her frowning after him.

Stephanie saw Troy being lifted from the bus and went over to check on him, glad he was finally out. She did his obs and smiled. 'You're doing just fine. How's the pain?'

'Not really there. Whatever you gave me has worked wonders.'

'I'm glad to hear it. It may be a while before you're transferred to the hospital so stay warm.' To add credence to her words, she tucked the blankets around him more tightly.

'Um…that girl you were with. Did she get out OK?'

'Yes. She's on her way to hospital. You rest.'

'Good advice.' Troy closed his eyes and sighed.

Stephanie checked in with the paramedic who was running the station platform triage. He directed her to more patients who needed her help.

When everything was finally under control at the platform, Oliver walked over to Stephanie's side. 'You all done?'

'Yes. What's next?'

'I think we'll head to the triage centre set-up at the health resort and leave the emergency crews to the clean up.'

'OK. I'll let David know.' Stephanie headed over to where the police rescue chief was having a much-needed cup of coffee and gave him the information. 'You've got my cellphone number if you need me. Just keep an eye on your crews. We have enough casualties at the moment and make sure they all get checked as well before they leave.'

'Will do. Go and check up on that brother of yours and make sure he's not getting into any trouble.' David grinned and then snapped his fingers. 'Oh, no. Wait a minute. *You're* the twin who gets into trouble, not him.'

'Funny.' She grinned as she handed over her hard hat and Oliver walked over. David peered inside the hat Stephanie had just taken off.

'Left any green bits behind?'

'Oh, you're a regular comedian tonight.'

David laughed and Stephanie joined in. She waited while Oliver handed over his own hat, noticing the frown was back on his face. Looked like Dr Jekyll was back, and she felt her own humour disappear. 'OK. We'll catch up with you later,' she said when Oliver was ready to go.

As they walked away from the accident site towards the health resort, they both remained silent. Stephanie's thoughts were jumbled as she tried to figure him out, and after a few minutes she threw her hands up in the air, deciding to just give up. If he wanted to be moody, then so be it.

'What?' Oliver asked.

'What, what?' she countered.

'You threw your hands up in the air.'

'So?'

He shrugged. 'OK. Forget it.'

'Forget what?' Stephanie was puzzled.

'Nothing.'

Stephanie shook her head, more confused than she'd been a few seconds ago. Before she could speak, however, he continued.

'Do you flirt with every man you come across?'

'I beg your pardon?' Stephanie was definitely affronted.

'Well, you were just flirting with David, you've been all over Stephen all night, and when we met a few hours ago, you were flirting with me.'

Stephanie stopped walking for a second and stared at him in disbelief. 'Oh, the ego,' she groaned. 'Here I thought you might be different from other doctors.'

Oliver stopped as well. 'What's that supposed to mean?'

She started walking faster than she had before, eager now to get to the health resort. 'Who says I was flirting? David and I have already dated and come to the conclusion we're better off as friends.'

Oliver scoffed with derision.

'What? What's the problem?' He opened his mouth to speak but she cut him off. 'I wasn't flirting with him, I was being friendly, and as for you…well…just because I think you're good-looking, that I initially found you funny and charming, it doesn't mean I'm ready to jump into bed with you!'

'What? I didn't think that at all.' She found him funny and charming? That was a start. Perhaps she wasn't as attached to her Stephen as he'd initially thought. Oliver shook his head as they walked up the front steps of the health resort. 'All I'm saying is that usually, once you're in a relationship, you shouldn't flirt with other men—even though you are very good at it,' he added with a groan.

Stephanie paused outside the door which lead to the triage centre. 'What are you talking about?'

'You and Stephen. How do you think he'd like it if he knew you'd been flirting with me or David?'

Stephanie felt warmth and excitement at his words. Did this mean Oliver found her attractive? It was on the tip of her tongue to tell him Stephen was her brother when anger hit. How dared he assume she'd act that way if she was in a relationship! That certainly summed up his impression of her and already he was acting as judge and jury in a situation he knew nothing about.

She opened her mouth to speak but shut it again, knowing anything she said to defend her behaviour would be misconstrued. And why should she *have* to defend herself? He was just her boss and colleague.

Instead, Stephanie shook her head and headed into the triage area, leaving Oliver to do whatever he wanted. At that moment she was past caring.

Triage on a massive scale wasn't something Stephanie was used to but she dealt with each case in turn and slowly but surely, as the hours passed, the area started to clear. People were either referred to Katoomba hospital for further treatment, or treated and told to see their GP within the next few days or attend a hospital clinic. Most of them had left the actual accident site with the more serious patients transferred to Sydney.

Between patients she just happened to glance over to where the resort had set up a tea and coffee area and saw Stephen and Nicolette talking to each other. They were smiling and getting along so well that a thrill of excitement coursed through her. Her brother was falling big time for the blonde doctor and Stephanie couldn't be happier. Nicolette headed back to her patients and Stephanie was about to go over and talk to her brother when she saw Oliver heading in his direction.

If Oliver thought she was dating Stephen *and* that she'd been flirting with other men, would he actually say something or was he still trying to figure things out? She watched the two of them, Stephen's back going ramrod straight, and she realised he'd slipped into 'protective big brother' mode. Even though he was only a few minutes older, he still counted himself as her *big* brother.

Neither of them offered a hand to shake in greeting and Stephanie had an immediate sense of apprehension as the two men appeared to be sizing each other up. She could see Stephen's expression more clearly than Oliver's and he was now speaking to her boss through gritted teeth. Stephanie bit her lip and stifled a nervous chuckle. Oh, this wasn't a good beginning at all. Perhaps she should have told Oliver the truth.

A moment later Oliver shrugged and walked away, glancing in her direction. She quickly turned her head and tried to focus on the piece of paper in front of her. Her next patient was a young teenage boy.

'Hi. I'm Stephanie. You must be Luke.'

'Yeah. Cool hair.'

'Thanks.' She sat next to him. 'I had it shaved off to raise money for cancer research.'

'Man, that's awesome. I've always wanted to get my head shaved but my parents won't let me.' Luke was eyeing her hair. 'What does it feel like? Is it really spiky?'

Stephanie laughed. 'Want to touch it?'

Luke's eyes widened in delight. 'Can I?'

'Sure.' Stephanie leaned forward and let him touch her short green spikes.

'Feels like little prickles but still soft. My hand's all tingly.'

'It's a few weeks since I had it shaved and it was more fuzzy before.'

'It's so awesome. Next time they do it, I'm definitely joining in.'

'You've got to raise the money, remember. That's what it's all about.'

'Yeah. Cool.'

'Anyway, Luke, what seems to be the problem tonight?'

'Apart from sitting here for ages?'

Stephanie chuckled. 'Sorry about that. Were you in the train?'

'Yeah, but in the back carriage. I hit my head and was really dizzy when I got out and I sat on the platform for a while before I was told to come here.'

Stephanie read his notes. He'd been assessed with a possible concussion and had been monitored during his time at the health resort. 'Well, it's certainly been a few hours since you bumped your head. How are you feeling now?'

'Not dizzy.'

'Are you here with anyone? Your parents?'

'My dad's already been taken to the hospital and my mum went with him. She said she'd come back to pick me up and I was to stay here until she did. That man over there...' he pointed to Oliver '...told her that was OK.'

'It's good to keep you quiet and still after a bump on the head. So were both your parents in the train?'

'Nah. Just me and my dad. I have a soccer training week in Sydney that starts tomorrow. Can I still go? Mum said no.'

'I don't think it's a good idea for you to be playing sport after a bad bump to your head. Let me have a look and we'll see what the situation is.' Stephanie took out the pen-light torch she'd nabbed not long after coming in the door. The hospital had sent down as many supplies as they could, but she knew if she put the torch down someone else would probably pick it up and she'd be left with nothing. 'I just want to look at your eyes, Luke.' She asked him to look in different directions as she performed his eye exam. 'Everything looks good there. Let's check your reflexes.' Again, he scored full marks. 'Exactly where did you bump your head? Can you show me?'

Luke put his hand to the back of his head and she stood and walked around to take a closer look. 'Excellent bump,' she praised. 'When you bump your head you do a good job. Nice one.'

Luke laughed a gawky teenage laugh. 'Cool.'

'So how old are you?'

'Thirteen and a half. Actually, I'm almost thirteen and three-quarters and the soccer clinic usually only takes boys who are fourteen and over, but my school coach said I'm talented so they accepted me early and now I'm not going to get to go.'

'I'm sorry, Luke. After a bump on the head like you've

had, we need to keep you quiet, at least for the next two weeks. You'll need to see your GP at that stage and even then you may need more time for your head to recover. I'm happy to write a note to the soccer clinic so they know it's not your fault, but how would you feel if you went down to play in the clinic and ended up having something else go wrong? You could end up in hospital for quite a few weeks and even need an operation.'

'Really?' Luke was astounded.

'I'm not trying to scare you but we treat head injuries very seriously. As I said, you've done an excellent job and you have quite a nice egg growing back there.'

'It hurts to touch it.'

'And it will. You'll also continue to get headaches for the next few weeks.'

'I've got a killer one now.'

'I'm not surprised.'

Luke looked over her shoulder. 'Mum!'

Stephanie turned around to see a woman, white-faced, rushing towards her son. 'Oh, darling, I'm sorry I've been so long. Are you all right?' She embraced her son and kissed him. Luke made a pathetic attempt to push her away, as all teenagers did, but Stephanie could see that he was relieved to have his mother back by his side again.

'How's Dad?' Luke's voice wobbled a bit as he asked the question.

'He's much better, darling. They've taken him to the ward as he's stable now.'

Stephanie introduced herself to Luke's mother. 'Luke's been a very lucky boy. He's sustained a mild concussion. He has good cognitive function and is showing positive signs of making a full recovery. However, I'd like him to go to the hospital tonight for X-rays. I know it's probably bedlam there but if you could wait, it would be better.

Chances are, the doctors will admit him even if it's just for observation overnight.'

'But you said he'll be all right?'

'Yes, but he needs to take it easy. No school for the next two weeks.'

'All right,' Luke interjected.

Stephanie turned and smiled at him. 'No music, no television, no games console, no computer, no mobile phone calls.' She ticked them off on her fingers. Luke's smile slid from his face. 'When I say take it easy for the next two weeks, I mean your brain needs a holiday. It needs time to heal.'

'And what about the sports clinic?' his mother asked.

'I've already discussed this with Luke. He's told me what an honour it was to be chosen, especially as he's not even fourteen.' Stephanie smiled at him. 'But strenuous activity after a concussion can have bad repercussions.'

Luke's mother nodded. 'So I can take him to the hospital?'

'Yes. If you require a medical certificate for the soccer clinic, let either myself or the doctor you see at the hospital know and we'll get that written out for you. Luke will also need to see your GP within two weeks but again it depends on what the X-rays show and the treatment he receives at the hospital. I can't stress enough how important it is that he's followed up.'

'I understand.' Luke's mother put her arm around her son and helped him up. 'Come on, sweetheart. Let's get you to the hospital. Thank you, Stephanie.'

'My pleasure. You take care, Luke.'

'I will.'

Stephanie signed off on Luke's notes before giving them to his mother and telling her to hand them in at the hospital. She then spent another hour seeing one patient after the next. After gulping down a much-needed cup of coffee, Oliver came over.

'I've just received word from the hospital that they need us back there. They're bursting at the seams with people, and as the crisis is now under control here it's time to go.'

'OK.' She was still a little angry with him but it had mellowed a bit. That didn't mean she was ready to let him off the hook. 'How do we get back to the hospital?'

'I've just spoken to one of the police officers and he'll give us a lift.'

'Sounds like a plan. Are you ready to go now?'

'Yes.'

'Okey-doke. Lead on, boss.' She smiled at him then frowned. 'Oops. Was I flirting with you then? Hmm. No. I don't think so. I was just talking. Is that all right?'

Oliver merely glowered at her and stalked out.

Stephanie walked over to the nurses' station to write up notes, surprised to find her brother sitting there, doing the same thing. She sank gratefully into a chair. 'What a night!'

'Agreed. I could have done without it, though.'

Stephanie brightened. 'Which reminds me, why were you and Nicolette first on the scene? Didn't Nic say you saw it happen?'

He didn't break from what he was writing, methodically finishing his work. He didn't have to say anything, Stephanie could read him like a book.

'You were going out, weren't you? The two of you. What was it? To celebrate her accepting the position as general practitioner in your new practice?'

'Something like that.'

'Ooh. How exciting.'

'Now, Steph.' He put his pen down and swivelled in the

chair to face her. 'Don't go getting all worked up about Nicolette and me. We're colleagues.'

'Yes, darling. Of course you are,' she said pacifyingly, and pinched his cheek. 'My only dilemma is whether to be chief bridesmaid or best man…or should that be best sister?'

'What's this best sister business? I only *have* one sister.'

'Exactly.' She preened. 'And I'm the best.'

Stephen laughed and stood, noticing Nicolette walking towards the nurses' station. 'Ready to go?' he asked.

'Yes,' Nicolette replied. 'If we're allowed out of here, that is.'

'Go,' Stephanie urged. 'Things are under control here…sort of.' She smiled tiredly at them. 'If we need you back, I'll call but for now, with the urgent cases being airlifted to Sydney and the majority of patients seen to, we're able to cope with what we have left.'

Nicolette glanced up at the clock. 'Is that the time?' She checked her watch.

Stephanie smiled. 'I've heard it flies when you're having fun.'

'Three o'clock? It's really three o'clock?'

'Time to at least get some sleep before you need to be at work later this morning,' Stephen said, indicating the door.

Stephanie stood and hugged her friend, then turned to face her brother. He had that stern, overly concerned expression on his face again. He gave her a hug. 'As it's your day off tomorrow, I'll expect you around for brunch. Eleven o'clock at the latest.'

Stephanie leaned her head on his shoulder for a second and then looked up at him. She drew so much strength from him and right now she needed all the reserves she could get. Not only to help her through the fatigue of the evening's events but also to deal with Oliver. 'I'll see you then.'

Stephen kissed her forehead. 'You be safe.'

'I will. Now go before something else happens.'

Oliver watched as Stephanie hugged first her friend, Nicolette, and then turned to face the man who had been uppermost in her mind all evening long. She hugged him close, resting her head on his shoulder, and Oliver was surprised at the tightening in his gut.

He still wasn't sure why he was having such a strong reaction to a woman he'd only just met, but he'd learned long ago to trust his instincts and his instinct wanted to know Stephanie Brooks a lot better.

When Stephen kissed her on the forehead, Oliver frowned. The least he'd expected had been a kiss on the lips—not some passionate clinch but more of a brief farewell before they parted. His gaze swung to Nicolette who was standing by the door, waiting for him. Come to think of it, the blonde doctor had stuck pretty closely to Stephen all night.

Oliver closed his eyes, unsure what type of mess he'd landed himself in. What he needed was sleep. Sleep in a nice warm bed. They were almost done here and all he needed to do was collect his suitcase from Stephanie's office—or, more correctly, *his* office—find out exactly where the house he'd rented was and then hopefully find the key in the letterbox as the estate agent had promised. He also hoped the house had instant heating because he was in no mood for lighting fires.

He opened his eyes and decided to get on with it. The sooner he was done, the sooner he could leave, and that meant taking a break from the beguiling presence of

Stephanie Brooks. He headed over to the nurses' station and sat in the chair Stephen had recently vacated.

Stephanie yawned.

'Go home,' he ordered.

'Really? You mean it?'

'No. I'm joking,' he replied, deadpan.

'Oh. OK. What's next, then?'

'Stephanie, I was teasing. Yes, I mean it. Go home.' The sooner she was out of his way, the better he'd cope, and right now he wasn't coping. How could his body react to her nearness at three o'clock in the morning? She had green hair, a lovely smile, a lovelier laugh and flirted with perfection. She was also taken, and if there was one thing he respected, it was monogamy. Pity his ex-wife hadn't had the same respect.

'Are you sure? I don't want you to think I'm leaving you in the lurch on your first day here.'

'It's not my first official day.'

'Yes, it is. It started three hours ago.' She pointed up at the clock.

'It's three o'clock?' he groaned. 'No wonder I feel so exhausted.'

'If anyone should go home, it should be you. You've travelled up from Sydney today.'

'Melbourne,' he corrected. 'I flew from Melbourne to Sydney, hired a car and drove here.'

'I rest my case—and now so should you. Go, Oliver. I think I can manage to hold the fort for a little longer.'

He nodded, deciding to let her win this round. When he went to stand up, she put out her hand to stop him. 'Before you go, though, there's something I need to clear up.'

He settled back into the chair, not sure he wanted to hear what she had to say. Now that he had permission to unwind, his mind was starting to shut down. Still, he waited patiently for her to speak.

'You seem to think Stephen and I are dating.'

'Believe me, the impression came across loud and clear.'

She smiled and he immediately felt the effect in his gut. Yes, even at three o'clock in the morning, she was dazzling. 'We're not dating.'

'I find that hard to bel—'

'Stephen's my brother.'

CHAPTER FOUR

IF SHE'D planned on shocking him, she'd done it. Scenes from the evening replayed through Oliver's mind. The way she'd spoken of him with love and fondness, the way Stephen had championed her talents, the way he'd been highly protective.

'We're twins, actually, which is why—'

'You felt claustrophobic when he was trapped.' Oliver nodded as the mental fog in his mind started to clear. 'I take it that means you're the type of twins who can sense each other.'

Stephanie nodded. 'It's a real pain sometimes.'

'The brother who buys you the earrings?'

She smiled, surprised—after everything that had happened—he'd remembered that inconsequential piece of information. 'That's right. He's also the only brother I have. My only sibling, actually.'

She wasn't dating Stephen. She wasn't dating Stephen! The words kept repeating themselves over and over in his dulled mind. 'Are you dating anyone else? You never did answer that question earlier.'

Butterflies churned in her stomach. Did that mean he was interested? She swallowed, feeling a little nervous. 'Uh… no. I'm currently unattached.'

Oliver nodded again, nice and slow, his gaze never leaving hers. 'So what's the story with Nicolette?'

'Nic?' Did he like the pretty blonde doctor? Stephanie swallowed the lump that had suddenly appeared in her throat. 'Nic is as interested in Stephen as he is in her. At

49

the moment, he's having a hard time admitting that, though.'

'Playing matchmaker?'

He didn't seemed bothered by the information and the lump began to vanish. Stephanie smiled. '*Moi?* Never!'

He returned her smile and stood looking down at her. 'Hmm. Why don't I completely believe you?'

She laughed. 'I have no idea, especially as you hardly know me.'

'I don't know if that's completely true,' he mumbled.

'Pardon?'

He shook his head. 'Nothing.' How could he possibly explain this…*sense* he seemed to have about her? Although it had been a very long night and he'd certainly learned many things about her, it didn't account for the feeling that he knew her a lot better.

Oliver put his hands in his pockets to stop himself from touching her, which is what he was becoming desperate to do. He'd seen young Luke touching her spiky hair and had felt a little jealous, wanting to reach out and touch it himself. He was also curious to find out what she'd looked like before she'd had her head shaved. Hadn't the CEO said she'd had red curls? He tried to picture her with hair like that but couldn't. Little green spikes and earrings. That was the picture that clearly defined Stephanie in his mind. That, mixed with the mild scent of vanilla. Together they made quite a heady combination.

And she wasn't dating Stephen. She was currently unattached.

Oliver tilted his head to the side as a thought struck him. 'Why didn't you tell me about Stephen sooner?' Stephanie opened her mouth to explain but he continued, answering his own question. 'You were peeved with me. I don't blame you. My behaviour was way out of line. So, to pay me back a little, you thought you'd string me along for a bit.'

'I had no idea you had jumped to those conclusions until we were outside the health resort.'

'Well, if you'd answered the question earlier, I wouldn't have jumped,' he countered, fatigue starting to get the better of him. It was all a storm in a teacup but he found it hard to control his reactions to this woman. She drew him in so completely he didn't know the difference between up or down. At the same time, she stirred his anger and rational thinking until it was a murky mess.

'So it's *my* fault?' she asked incredulously. 'You're blaming me for not telling you my life story the instant we met?'

Oliver exhaled harshly and raked a hand through his hair, pushing the lock back from his forehead the way he'd done when she'd met him. 'I apologise again, Stephanie. I didn't mean to imply that at all. Look, I think we both need some sleep.' And time to think things through, he added silently.

'Agreed.' Her tone was soft.

Still, he didn't move. He stood where he was, not moving, their gazes locked. Tension spiralled through her, her heart rate increased and her mouth went dry. Her reaction to him was immediate and by the way his eyes were darkening with desire, it was obvious he felt that same attraction. Never before had a man been able to affect her so easily and yet so powerfully as Oliver could. It scared and thrilled her at the same time.

Her tongue came out to wet her lips and she swallowed, trying to moisten her throat. 'You do feel that, don't you?'

Although her words were soft, his gut tightened and the urge to touch her increased. 'Yes.'

At the single-word admission, she nodded and allowed a slow sigh to escape her parted lips. 'Thank goodness. I didn't want it to be just a figment of my imagination.'

'It's not.'

His deep voice washed over her and she loved the way

it made her feel, all warm and feminine and mushy inside. Their gazes still seemed locked, impatient for them to move things forward, but they both knew that couldn't happen— not yet. 'What do we do about it?'

Oliver took her hand in his, unable to resist the temptation any longer. She gasped at the contact, goose-bumps spreading up her arm and over her body. 'We get some sleep, we slow it down and we get to know each other.'

Her smile encompassed him once more. 'Good answer.' Unwilling to break the contact straight away, she held firmly to his hand as she rose to her feet. She was buzzing on instinct as she leaned forward and pressed a soft kiss to his cheek. 'Mmm, you smell so nice.'

'So do you.' He closed his eyes for a second, savouring the moment. The feel of her lips against his roughened jaw, her scent as it entwined itself about him. He wanted to grab her to him, press his lips to hers and plunder her mouth to the very depths of her being. Instead, he continued to savour. She may be direct and forthright, it didn't mean she wasn't vulnerable beneath her happy-go-lucky exterior.

She chuckled. 'You think so? Even after the hectic day we've had?' She shifted back and met his gaze once more, their hands still clasped between them. 'I think I'm in serious need of a shower.'

'No. You smell…delicious.'

'Good enough to eat, eh? Must be the vanilla essence I dabbed on this morning.'

'Vanilla essence?'

'Complaints?' She raised her eyebrows, happy and excited to be back in the 'flirting zone' with Oliver. She could cope in the flirting zone. She knew what the rules were and how to use them to her best advantage.

'No. No. Not at all,' he quickly assured her, giving her hand another squeeze before he reluctantly let go. Stephanie sank down into the chair again, glad of its support as she knew there was no way her legs were going to do the trick.

'Go and find your new home, Oliver.'

He continued to look at her and it was ten seconds before he moved. Finally, he shifted and the bubble they'd been caught up in was broken. 'Good advice. Can I borrow your key to the office? I need my suitcase.'

'Of course. I'd completely forgotten.' She shifted, not trusting her legs just yet, and pulled the key-card from her pocket. 'Don't worry about returning it. I'm going to finish up here and head home.'

'You don't need it to get your bag or keys? You did leave them in there, didn't you?'

She waved his concerns away. 'I'll get Security to let me in. Connor, the security guard on tonight, will have to walk me to my car anyway. Take it and go.'

'Glad to hear this hospital employs the correct safety protocols.'

'My house—before it burnt down—wasn't that far from here, and on occasions the security guys used to walk me all the way home.'

'Just like the last little piggy?' He ignored the feeling of jealousy at the thought of other men ensuring her safety. The urge to protect her himself was becoming more overwhelming with every moment he spent in her company. Which was proof that he should go… But he couldn't. He wanted to stay here, to talk with her, to find out more about her…to see her safely home himself. Surely she wouldn't be much longer. He could wait.

Stephanie smiled. 'Yes, except, I don't go "wee, wee, wee". Go and rest. You're starting to look very tired.'

He raised his eyebrows. 'Is that so?'

'Yes, it is. Now go and let me finish up here.'

'Am I distracting you, Dr Brooks?'

'Yes, as a matter of fact, you are. Now go.' She waved her hand in the air, effectively dismissing him.

It was on the tip of his tongue to say he'd wait for her when Sophie walked over to where they were and slumped down into a chair. 'What a night.'

'You can say that again.' Stephanie grinned. 'Not a nice initiation for poor Oliver.'

'Poor Oliver,' he drawled as he moved away, 'has survived much worse than tonight.'

'Get going. We're scheduled to be hitting the paperwork in your new office in a few hours' time, so go.'

'I've survived paperwork before, too.'

'Oh, will you just go and leave us in peace?' She laughed. 'I've never seen a doctor so reluctant to leave the hospital before.'

'All right. I'm going, I'm going.' He smiled at both women. 'See you later today.'

Both women watched him walk away and then turned to look at each other.

'Mmm-mmm. He's a nice one,' Sophie said. 'I'm not one to drool over the doctors, like Lauren, but he's definitely a nice one.'

'No argument from me.' They gave a mutual sigh then smiled. 'I'd better finish up or I'll still be here when Oliver comes back.'

Sophie laughed. 'Then let's finish up what you need to do so you, too, can get some rest.' Half an hour later Stephanie had finished her work, showered quickly and changed into the spare clothes she kept in her locker and was being walked to her car by Connor, the security guard. He was pushing fifty, a little overweight but would certainly be able to defend her against unwanted persons if necessary.

'You drive carefully,' he warned her. 'You look dead on your feet.'

'It's not far but I promise I won't close my eyes until I'm tucked up in bed.'

'Good girl.' He smiled at her before shutting her car door and waiting until she'd started the engine. As she drove carefully through the fog, she wondered whether she had the energy to make a pot of relaxing herbal tea or whether just brushing her teeth and lying down would be better.

As usual, she headed into the small back lane behind the house, rather than heading in the front way which was off a rather busy side street. She parked her car, climbed out and locked it. She was surprised when the outside sensor light didn't come on but brushed the thought away, rationalising she'd accidentally switched it off when she'd last left the house.

Stephanie unlocked the door and headed inside, deciding tea was first on her list. She headed to the kitchen, switching on the light and dumping her bag, coat and scarf onto the bench before filling the kettle.

A loud yell rang through the house and she immediately switched off the tap, trembling. What was that? Her heart was pounding wildly as she put the kettle down and walked quickly over to her bag, reaching for her cellphone. She dialled Stephen's number, her finger on the 'connect' button as she slowly walked up the corridor, flicking on lights as she went.

As she neared the bathroom, she heard the sound of taps being switched off. Had someone broken into her house just to have a shower? It was then she realised she hadn't forgotten to switch the sensor light on. Someone else had switched it off. Her mind started racing. If whoever it was had wanted to hurt her, she doubted they'd be in the shower.

The immediate threat she'd felt disappeared but now there was only confusion. Still, with her finger poised and ready on her cellphone, she called, 'Who's there?'

She stood in the hallway, just outside the bathroom door and waited. 'Hello?'

A moment later the door was wrenched open and she jumped back in fright. Her hand covered her mouth as she bit back a scream. Steam floated out and a man, clad only in a black towel, stood before her…wet legs, knobbly knees and all.

Stephanie's gaze met his and her eyes widened in total shock. Her jaw went slack and for a moment she was totally incapable of speech or thought.

'Stephanie!' Oliver's eyes were as wide as her own. He was as much in shock as she was but had found his voice first. 'What are you doing in my house?'

'*Your* house?'

'Yes. Well, no.' He closed his eyes for a moment as though trying to shut her out. He opened them just as quickly. 'Er…the house I'm renting.'

'You're *renting* this place?' She felt a prickle of uneasiness ripple over her entire body. 'Oh-h,' she groaned, her stomach churning itself into knots.

'Yes. What's the matter? Are you ill?'

'No.' There'd been a mix-up. Her friend who owned the house had obviously not informed the estate agency that the place was now occupied. She frowned. Or perhaps she was supposed to have done that. 'Oh-h,' she groaned again. 'I need to sit down.' She turned and walked back to the lounge room, dropping her phone onto the coffee-table. She allowed the comfortable wing-backed chair to envelop her as she brought her feet up so she could hug her knees. 'What a mess,' she whispered, her eyes closed almost in agony. Not only was she now sharing a house with Oliver Bowan, she had the electric vision of him clad only in a towel to add to her ever-increasing bank of memories. How was she supposed to fight any attraction to him when he was so close…and not even dressed?

The thought of sliding her fingers over his broad shoulders, down his firm torso, which was covered in a fine layer of dark hair, and whipping that towel away made her almost hyperventilate.

'Stephanie?'

Her eyes snapped open at the sound of his voice and she worked hard to control her breathing as the man himself came into view. This time, thankfully, he was at least partly clothed, the pair of well-worn denim jeans moulded to his shape, outlining his firm thigh muscles which had previously been hidden beneath the towel. In fact, Stephanie wasn't sure what was worse. Oliver, wet and clad in only a towel, or in form-fitting denim, his torso bare. Either vision was one she was willing to ponder upon for quite some time, but how did she cope with the emotions they evoked?

She swallowed and simply stared, losing the fight to get her shallow breathing under control, let alone her self-control. He pulled on a creased T-shirt as he bent to sit in the chair opposite her. She couldn't control the sigh that escaped her lips as his body was hidden from further view.

'Stephanie?' She forced herself to meet his gaze and found him frowning at her. 'Are you all right?'

She tried to nod but wasn't sure how successful she was. Thankfully, she'd managed to close her mouth so she didn't look so much like the drooling fool she was.

'I know you've had a fright but it's OK. We can work this out.' He raked a hand through his wet hair, making it stand on end even more than before. She couldn't help the smile that touched her lips.

'This is funny?' he asked.

'No.' The word didn't come out too well and she cleared her throat. 'No,' she said firmly, but the smile didn't disappear. 'Your hair…' She pointed. 'It's kind of standing on end.' He quickly went to flatten it down again. 'No. It looks cute.'

'Cute? Stephanie, we have a major dilemma here and all you can think is that I look cute?'

Her smile increased and she raised her eyebrows. 'Something wrong with that?'

'Stop teasing. This is serious.'

She made a concentrated effort to pull her features into a somewhat serious expression. Oliver rolled his eyes and stood. 'Well, I'll be the serious one here. You can just make jokes.'

Stephanie chuckled as she watched him pace, barefoot, up and down in front of her. Oh, yes, he was *very* cute and getting cuter by the second. 'Oliver. Sit down. It's all right. As you've legally rented this house, I'll stay here the night and then move in with Stephen until I can find somewhere else.'

'No. Don't say that. You make me feel as though I'm turfing you out in the cold.' He paused and thought for a moment. 'You've been through your own troubles, with your house burning down and then moving here.'

'Honestly, Oliver, it's not as though I have a lot of stuff to move. Stephen won't mind.' But even as she said the words, she frowned. Stephen had offered her his spare room when the fire had happened but after the first week of being with him, she'd opted out. His life was very precarious at the moment and she knew if she stayed with him longer, it might damage the relationship he was building with Nicolette. There was no way she was going to jeopardise that. Her brother's need for happiness was long overdue and she was certain Nicolette could provide it. No. She couldn't move back in with Stephen but Oliver didn't need to know that.

'Why are you frowning?'

She quickly changed her expression. 'Nothing. It's fine.' She put her legs on the floor and went to stand, but found that her body wasn't yet ready to follow commands. She settled back. 'I'll be gone first thing in the morning…or later today as it's just after four o'clock.'

'No. Stop. Just wait. There's no reason for you to move. I was planning on moving soon anyway. This place was just a stopgap for a few weeks until I could find permanent housing. It'll take months until your home is rebuilt.'

'What? Are you saying we should share?'

Oliver shrugged. 'Why not? I've shared houses with other female colleagues before…during med school and strictly platonic,' he added.

Stephanie nodded slowly. She, too, had been in a group house, sharing with both males and females, during med school. Of course, one of the men had been her brother but that hadn't made any difference. They'd all been coming and going at all sorts of hours and chances were, with Oliver taking over the new director's position at the hospital, he'd be the one working the longer hours. Longer hours working out those hateful rosters! She couldn't help grinning at the thought but then turned her thoughts to the issue at hand.

'If we do decide to do this, then you shouldn't have to pay rent. The fact that I'm already in the house as a guest means that you should be here under the same conditions.'

'I'm more than happy to pay.'

'It's all right. My friend won't mind. He's very generous.'

'He?' Oliver raised a questioning eyebrow, then said quickly, 'Forget it. It's none of my business.'

Stephanie smiled. 'His name is Gregor and he and his wife bought this house when Stephen and I were about two years old. He is also our godfather so, honestly, Oliver, I doubt he'd insist on payment when he hears of the mix-up. If anything, I'm the one that should be paying to rent this house as I think it was my responsibility to notify the estate agency that I'd moved in.'

'I guess you've had a lot on your mind.'

She nodded. 'I guess I have.' She tried to stand again and was thankful that this time her legs seemed willing to co-operate with the signals her brain was sending. 'So it's settled, then. We'll just stay here and share the house until you find a more permanent residence.'

Oliver slowly shook his head.

'What now?'

'There is one other spanner I'd like to throw into the works.'

'Oh?' Stephanie reached out and placed a hand on the arm of the chair. Was he going to mention the undeniable attraction between them again? Would they be able to fight it? They'd just have to, she rationalised. It was only for a few weeks and they'd both be busy at the hospital. She waited for him to speak, watching again as he raked his hand through his hair, a smile automatically twitching at her lips. Yes. Definitely cute.

'It's my daughter.'

Stephanie's eyes were once again open wide, staring at Oliver. 'You have a *daughter*?'

'Yes. She's eight and she's due here on Wednesday evening.' He stopped and groaned. 'That's tomorrow. I came on ahead to try and get things organised.'

Stephanie sank back down into the chair as her legs gave way. Oliver had a daughter! She shook her head as though the equation didn't compute.

'My ex-wife, Nadele, hasn't played fair with the custody of Kasey since we divorced six years ago. This time, though, with me moving back to Australia, she put up all sorts of fights because I wanted to take Kasey out of the country. The fact that Nadele doesn't even want Kasey around has nothing to do with it. She just doesn't want me to have her.' He was speaking more to himself than to her and the way his eyes had darkened with pain and disgust surprised Stephanie. Up until then, she'd seen Oliver in several moods but this hadn't been one of them.

'What does Kasey want to do?' she ventured quietly.

'Kasey? She's only eight.'

'So? Eight-year-olds do have minds of their own, Oliver.'

'You don't know anything about the situation,' he remarked, brushing her words away.

'You're right. I don't.' Stephanie tried not to be hurt at his words. It was quite true. She hardly knew anything about him and nothing at all about custody battles over eight-year-old girls. This isn't your problem, she told herself firmly, and this time forced her legs to comply as she stood.

'I'm heading to bed. I guess I'll see you…later. Goodnight, Oliver.'

'Wait.' He put out a hand to her but she stepped away. 'I'm sorry, Stephanie. I didn't mean to snap.'

'It's fine. It's been a very long introduction to life in the Blue Mountains for you. Let's get some rest and discuss things later.'

He exhaled sharply and nodded. 'You're right. Sleep well.'

She smiled politely and headed up the corridor. 'Yeah, right,' she mumbled to herself as she entered her room and shut the door. She flopped down onto the mattress, kicking off her shoes. Oliver had a daughter. It certainly altered the picture she'd drawn of him. Busy doctor, doting dad. She had a lot of unanswered questions. When Kasey arrived, what did he plan on doing with her while he was at work? Was she attending school here or staying for an extended period of time?

Surely Oliver didn't need a woman around to help him

deal with his daughter? Was that the reason he wanted her to stay while Kasey was here?

But the question at the top of her list was why no one had asked the eight-year-old girl what *she* wanted. Did she even want to come to Australia? Life here was very different from Seattle, USA, especially as Kasey was probably enjoying summer vacation, while here it was cold, foggy and probably—to an eight-year-old—miserable, dull and boring.

'It's nothing to do with you,' she told herself. 'Not your problem,' she reiterated, and tried to get up off the bed and change before she fell asleep in her clothes. Her limbs felt so heavy it was easier to just snuggle beneath the covers and close her eyes, thoughts of Oliver mixing with a picture of what his daughter might look like.

It seemed as though she'd just closed her eyes when a sound made her sit bolt upright in bed. Someone was in her house! Then she remembered about Oliver. Stephanie glanced across at the bedside clock and was surprised to find it was just after half past eight. She yawned and stretched before swinging her legs over the side of the bed. Slipping her feet into warm, fleece ugg-boots, she opened the door and headed out to the kitchen.

'Mmm. Coffee,' she mumbled sleepily.

'Bacon and eggs?'

'Mmm,' she murmured again. 'Sounds great, although with you coming from America I'd have expected flapjacks and grits.'

'But I'm not American. I'm Australian, remember.'

'Oh, yes.' She poured herself a cup and shuffled around to the other side of the kitchen bench, perching on one of the stools. After her first sip of the rich, black liquid, she sighed and slumped forward onto the bench. 'Need any help?' came her muffled question.

'Ha. Like you're in a state to help.'

She lifted her head and gazed at him through bleary eyes. 'I'll have you know I can do a lot of things in this state.' The instant the words were out of her mouth, she regretted them. They may both be exhausted and fatigued but the *double entendre* hung in the air like a hummingbird. For a split second she saw Oliver's gaze darken slightly, as though he knew exactly what he wanted her to be capable of.

He swallowed and forced himself to turn away, to concentrate on cooking breakfast before he burnt it. Why had her innocent remark left him feeling as though he'd like nothing better than to scoop her up and carry her back to her warm bed? Perhaps sharing the house with her wasn't such a good idea after all.

'How do you like your eggs?' he asked, disgusted by the desire he heard in his own tone. He glanced over his shoulder only to find her grinning, her blue eyes filled with mirth. 'What?'

'Nothing, nothing. Er…scrambled.'

'You've got that right,' he muttered, thinking both their minds had been scrambled ever since they'd met. He'd fought several different emotions since crossing paths with Stephanie, but the desire between them was highly evident.

'I meant the eggs, Oliver,' she remarked, as though she could read his mind. 'If we're going to share this house, we might need to set down some ground rules.'

'We won't need too many,' he ventured. 'Mrs Dixon is flying to Australia with Kasey. Now, Mrs Dixon,' he went on before she could question him, 'was my family's housekeeper and sort of nanny when my brother and I weren't at boarding school. She retired when my father died but I was able to persuade her to look after Kasey during her

Australian visit, otherwise Nadele wouldn't have consented to the visit.'

'Ah. I had wondered what would become of Kasey when you were at work.'

'Mrs Dixon is very, shall we say, strict, so she'll make a perfect chaperone for us as well as ensuring your virtue remains intact.'

Stephanie couldn't help it. She threw back her head and laughed. 'Oh, Oliver. You're priceless. Were you sent to an all-boys, stiff-upper-lip school?'

'In Sydney, yes. Does it show?' He grinned back at her.

'Only sometimes.' She watched as he finished scrambling the eggs and making toast. 'Look, perhaps it's better if I just move out. It's no big deal and—'

'No. As I said a few hours ago, you've been through enough trauma.'

'I bounce.' She shrugged as though it were nothing.

'I can see through your nonchalance, Stephanie.' His tone was deep and caring, his gaze said he understood. In that split second Stephanie felt tears well behind her eyes. How could he do this to her? One minute she was laughing and the next she was crying. 'You're more fragile than you let on. I'm surprised your brother hasn't picked up on it.'

'He has,' she replied, not denying his words. 'He also knows not to smother me.'

Oliver dished up the meal he'd cooked and put a plate of food in front of her. 'Am I smothering you?'

She looked down at the plate and then gasped in horror, then relaxed again.

'What?'

'I just remembered I was supposed to go to Stephen's place for brunch but that's not until eleven o'clock.'

'Eleven o'clock?' He frowned for a moment. 'Is it your day off today?'

'Yes. You think I'd learn to sleep in but I just can't.'

'I know the feeling. Well, you can't survive without food until then. Eat.'

'Don't you worry, I intend to.' She grinned as she picked up her fork. 'After all, it's not every day my new boss cooks me breakfast. Thanks.'

'You're welcome.' He collected one of the bench stools and took it around to the kitchen side so they could eat opposite each other. 'That's another point. Perhaps it shouldn't be general knowledge around the hospital that we're sharing accommodation.'

Stephanie swallowed her mouthful. 'Why not?'

'Because then people would think that we're...you know.' He shrugged.

'But Mrs Dixon will be here, remember?'

'But still.'

'Oliver, it won't work. Katoomba is small enough so people will find out anyway and it's better to openly admit what's happened as an honest mix-up and that we're dealing with the situation like professional colleagues.'

'They won't believe it.'

She shrugged. 'Their problem. Besides, it does have added compensations for you.'

Again that tinge of desire sparked briefly in his eyes but she waved it away. 'Not *those* compensations.' She smiled shyly and shook her head, wondering how far she could push him and how much information she'd be able to discover. 'It will keep people like Lauren from throwing herself at you. That is, unless you *want* women like Lauren throwing themselves at you, in which case I'm happy to—'

'No. No, thanks. I've encountered the Laurens of this world—no offence to any of them, well, except perhaps Nadele—and I have no desire to repeat my mistakes.'

Stephanie breathed an inward sigh of relief, glad the perky brunette wasn't his type.

'I am a changed man,' he announced proudly. 'Reformed from falling for women who are stunning yet shallow, divine yet dishonest.'

'Pretty yet…piranha-ish?' she couldn't resist adding.

He smiled. 'Exactly.'

'Whew!' She pretended to wipe her brow. 'I'm glad I'm none of those things.'

As Oliver's smile slowly disappeared, he held her gaze. 'No.' The word was soft yet definite. 'You're not.' Without breaking eye contact, he slowly shook his head. 'You're so different, Stephanie.'

Warmth flooded her at his words and she parted her lips to allow a rush of air to escape between her lips. She felt feminine and cherished, just from the way he was looking at her. She felt shy and coy, which wasn't like her at all, and it was all thanks to the man before her.

Her gaze flicked down to his mouth as he continued to speak.

'You're a woman who doesn't care if she sleeps in her clothes. When you shake your head, your earrings make a cute tinkling noise.' The corners of his mouth had started to curve into a smile as he spoke, and she had to admit she was mesmerised by his look, his mouth but most of all his words. 'And you have all your hair shaved off for a good cause,' he concluded, drawing in a deep breath and slowly exhaling. 'Add to that the fact that you are stunning…' he reached out and pushed his plate of food to the side '…deliciously divine…' he leaned a little closer '…and perfectly pretty, not to mention incredibly sexy.' He took her hand in his and gently rubbed his thumb in little caressing circles.

She was finding it difficult to swallow, to speak, to think!

Never, in her life, had a man said anything more…romantic to her.

'When do Kasey and Mrs Dixon arrive?' She wasn't surprised to find her voice husky with repressed emotion.

Oliver swallowed as he leaned further across the bench, pushing her plate of food aside as well. Stephanie leaned in, too, eagerly closing the gap between them.

'Not soon enough,' he growled before pressing his lips firmly to hers.

CHAPTER FIVE

STEPHANIE'S insides whirled with nervous anticipation as her eyelids fluttered closed so she could savour the moment.

She loved first kisses and although she'd kissed Oliver at the hospital earlier that morning, it had been merely an acknowledgement that she was attracted to him, rather than following through on that attraction.

Now, though, she let the emotions flood her body, thrilled with each and every one of them. His warm lips remained pressed to hers for a few more seconds as the heightened tension between them began to change from one of repression to one of expression. Through touch, they could express the growing feelings both had been trying to deal with since they'd first met less than twenty-four hours ago.

She breathed in and sighed as his warm, spicy scent swirled around her, helping to create the world that held only the two of them. He was once more fresh from the shower and she found she could quite easily become addicted to him. Whether that was a good thing was yet to be decided.

For the moment she concentrated on how it felt to finally have his mouth pressed to hers, and just as she became accustomed to the tingles spreading throughout her entire body, his lips parted slightly, his touch slow and light but, oh, so seductive, causing a new wave of tingles to assail her senses.

A few more kisses before a groan of what she hoped was sheer pleasure came from deep within him and he gently slipped his tongue between her lips. The pressure became a bit more intense but he didn't change pace even though his exploration was becoming more thorough.

She'd had no idea she could feel this way from just a kiss. Letting him lead, she willingly followed, eager to learn. It was as though he was now acting out his previous words. He'd said he found her incredibly sexy and, thanks to his masterful mouth, she now felt incredibly sexy. It was an amazing feeling.

He pulled back slightly, allowing them each a moment to take a breath before he brushed his lips over hers a few more times. Again, she couldn't control the sigh that flowed through her, her body temperature still rising as he brought one hand up to cup her cheek.

With a regret she could almost feel, he pulled back and she slowly opened her eyes. Why had he stopped? Had she done something wrong? Should she tell him that she wasn't as experienced at the 'romance' game as he probably thought she was? Anxiety began to well up within her in that one split second but as soon as her gaze encountered his and she saw the burning desire still evident in his blue depths, her fears were washed away.

'Wow,' he whispered, and again she felt shyness creep over her. She knew she wasn't anything super-special but with the words he'd said and the kiss they'd just shared, maybe Oliver didn't share that opinion. Perhaps she *was* super-special after all.

A small smile touched her lips and she looked away for a moment, trying to cope with the swell of feminine power he was making her feel. She'd seen other women use their feminine wiles to bring otherwise unsuspecting males to their knees, but she'd never experienced it before. Not that she'd brought Oliver to his knees, far from it. He'd been the one driving what they'd just shared, but the fact that he'd been unable to resist her was something she found both thrilling and stimulating.

'Steph?'

She raised her gaze to meet his once more but gasped when he brushed his thumb across her lips and back again, her chest rising and falling quickly as her heart rate began to pick up once more.

'You respond so ardently to my touch. It's as though you've been made for me and me for you,' he murmured, and as though unable to help himself, he leaned forward and once more pressed his mouth to hers. Stephanie closed her eyes again, ready for another onslaught, almost desperate for him to take her higher than he had only moments ago, but after two quick kisses he pulled back, dropped his hands from her and stepped backwards. Her eyes snapped open in confusion.

'This is not good.'

Again anxiety began to well within her. 'It isn't?'

'Steph, don't look at me like that or I won't be held accountable for my lack of self-control.'

His words slowly sank in. He wasn't rejecting her, he was trying to control his desire for her. Another surge of feminine power washed over her and she smiled, breathing a sigh of relief.

'It's pretty powerful, isn't it,' she stated rhetorically.

Oliver raked his hand through his hair and nodded. 'Yeah.'

'Perhaps I shouldn't stay here.'

Oliver looked down at the floor and slowly exhaled, as though still trying to get himself under control. 'Let's just let the haze lift and wait for rational thought to return. We can figure this out, Stephanie. I know we can.' As though to prove it to himself as well as her, he reached over and took the plate he'd previously placed in front of her. 'Let me warm this up.'

After he'd set it in the microwave, the phone rang and Stephanie automatically reached over to scoop the cordless phone from its cradle. 'Dr Brooks.'

'Oh. I'm so sorry. I think I have the wrong number.' The female voice that spoke was very English with well-enunciated words.

'Who were you after?'

'I was looking for Dr Oliver Bowan.'

'You've called the correct number. He's right here.' She held out the phone to Oliver.

He frowned, trying to figure out who it was. Several people had his Katoomba contact details. One person was his ex-wife and right now, with the imprint of Stephanie's lips firmly on his, Nadele was the last person he wanted to speak to. He cleared his throat and took the receiver. 'Dr Bowan.'

Not wanting to eavesdrop on his conversation, Stephanie picked up her mug of coffee from the bench and stood.

'Mrs D.,' he said quickly, his frown disappearing and a smile spreading across his face. 'Good to hear from you.' He motioned for Stephanie to sit back down, and when the microwave beeped he took her plate out and set it in front of her.

'Eat,' he whispered, before turning his attention back to his phone call. 'I take it you're safely in the States?'

'Yes, dear. I'll be collecting Kasey in about three hours' time and then we'll head off to the airport.'

'I've arranged for transport once you arrive in Sydney to bring you up to Katoomba.'

'You said that would add another two hours to our journey, correct?'

'Yes, but the car I've arranged is comfortable enough so you'll both be able to sleep if necessary.'

'She *is* going to be awfully tired, Oliver. You know that,

don't you? When she arrives it will take her a few days to get over her jet-lag.'

'I realise that. I've asked Nadele to take her to the doctor so a travel sickness sedative can be prescribed. The last time I went on a car trip with Kasey, she was quite ill.'

'But she was only two years old, dear.'

'Don't remind me. It was the worst vacation I've ever had and the straw that broke the camel's back as far as my marriage went.'

'Well, that was all a long time ago and water under the bridge. I'll contact Nadele now just to make sure she's actually done as you've asked. Knowing that woman, she probably hasn't and I don't want young Kasey being sick. This should be a fun experience for her.'

'I certainly hope so.' He sounded gloomy.

'She doesn't want to come to Australia?'

'She wants to come. Whether she wants to see me or not is another matter.' Oliver shook his head.

'Things still aren't good between the two of you?'

'It depends on how much Nadele has poisoned her mind against me.'

'She's an intelligent little girl, Oliver. She'll realise the truth as she gets older.'

'Thanks, Mrs D.' Oliver tried to focus on something else rather than the strained relationship he currently had with his daughter. The poor child felt very unloved and un-wanted, at least that was the impression he'd received two weeks ago when he'd last seen her. He hoped this trip to Australia, where her mother wouldn't be around to cause friction between them, might actually help to restore some sort of balance in Kasey's life. If he had his way—if Nadele would give in—Kasey would be living permanently with him in Australia where he hoped they could start a new life together.

He picked up his plate of cold food and put it in the

microwave. 'I'll see you tomorrow evening when you arrive. Call me if there are any hiccups.'

'I will, dear. Bye-bye.'

Oliver ended the call and replaced the phone in its cradle before placing both hands on the bench and pressing on his arms, his head hanging, his eyes closed. This needed to work, he prayed. Kasey needed to like it here and Nadele needed to give in and relinquish her claim on their daughter. It wasn't right for the child. She needed stability, not to feel as though she was a prize possession being fought over by parents she thought didn't even want her.

'You OK?' Stephanie forked in another mouthful of eggs. Oliver lifted his head and looked at her for a moment. She was surprised at the hurt and vulnerability reflected in his eyes. She chewed and quickly swallowed. 'Oliver?'

'My daughter hates me.' The four words seemed to be wrenched from deep down inside him and Stephanie frowned.

'She may think she does but from what I overheard, her mother has a lot to answer for regarding your daughter's attitude.'

'You asked last night what Kasey wants and I said she doesn't know what she wants. That's not really true. She doesn't want to spend time with either of her parents. When I last saw her, she told me she'd be far happier spending her summer vacation hanging around the boarding school and helping the grounds staff out. Can you believe that? She'd rather spend her summer with strangers than her own father.'

'Do you think forcing her to come here and spend time with you is the answer?'

'I don't know, but it was all I could think of. Getting her away from Nadele's clutches was another motive. Nadele said she'd planned to visit Kasey at school but, knowing Nadele, she'd raise the poor child's hopes and then dash them by not showing up at all.' He shook his head and exhaled sharply. 'I'm sorry. This isn't your problem.'

'Oliver, perhaps it's better if I'm not in the house. I mean, she'll be here in a foreign environment, and having a complete stranger in the house might not be the best thing. I can go stay somewhere else. Sorting things out with your daughter is important.'

He surprised her by smiling. 'Genuinely giving as well. The more I get to know about you, Dr Stephanie Brooks, the more I like you. Listen, I didn't honestly think about this last night when I suggested we share the house, but since then the idea has grown on me. Having you in the house might actually be good for Kasey. As you said, you're a stranger and at the moment she seems to get along better with strangers than with her parents.' He grimaced. 'She knows Mrs Dixon but more in a disciplinarian role. With you, she might actually be able to relax and unwind.'

'That's putting quite a bit of pressure on me.'

'I know, and that's why I wanted to mention it now. You don't owe me anything, Steph. We're colleagues...' He shrugged. 'Hopefully we're becoming friends...maybe more, given the attraction we both feel, but, still, you don't owe me anything and I completely understand if you'd rather not be here.'

Stephanie drained her coffee-cup. 'I need to think about it.' What she needed to do was to discuss things with Stephen. Her brother had the knack of making her feel more in control and right now that's what she needed because Oliver made her feel totally out of control.

'Good decision.' He nodded as the microwave beeped.

'Thanks for breakfast,' she said, scooting off the stool. 'It was delicious.'

'You're going to leave me to eat alone?'

She smiled. 'I think you need to think as well. I'm going

to have a shower so when you're finished we can head off to the hospital to get some paperwork done.' She started out of the room but stopped when he called her name.

'But today's your day off. I'll manage.'

'It's OK. As I wasn't expecting you until the weekend, I thought it best to roster myself off during the week so I was available to help you when you arrived.'

'Sorry to ruin your plans.'

'You haven't ruined them. So long as I get to have brunch with my brother, I can work around that.'

'Hopefully, you'll be able to take some time off on the weekend.'

She shook her head. 'That would mean changing the roster.'

'So?'

Stephanie levelled him with a glare. 'We are not changing the roster!'

Oliver held up his hands in defence. 'Fine. The roster stays as it is.'

'Good.' She straightened her shoulders. 'Now, eat your breakfast. I'll be ready to leave in ten minutes.'

'Ten minutes?' he scoffed as she headed down the corridor. 'A woman ready in ten minutes. I'd like to see that.' He laughed to himself as he took his plate out of the microwave.

True to her word, she was standing waiting for him ten minutes later, her coat on, a colourful scarf wrapped around her neck and her bag in her hands. 'It's probably best if we each take our own car. That way you can stay at the hospital for as long as you need to. Do you have the hospital key-card?'

Oliver searched around for where he'd left his keys the previous night and found it on top of the refrigerator. 'Here it is.'

'Good. Ready?'

'Just let me get my coat.' He wandered down to his room but returned a second later, carrying his coat over his arm, his briefcase in hand. 'Don't you need a hat or something for your head? I imagine it could get quite cold.'

'Yes. I'm surprised how much cooler the wind feels. That was a sensation I was unprepared for,' Stephanie chattered as they left the house, locking the door behind them. 'I usually do wear a hat but it's supposed to be a whole two degrees warmer today so I'll see how I go.'

She walked towards the back of the house.

'Where are you going?' he asked, totally bewildered.

'I parked around here. I usually do. There's a little alleyway one street down and it's easier to get in and out of rather than chancing the busy street out front.'

'Is there room for both our cars out back?'

'Yes.' She fished her keys out and jangled them on her finger, feeling a little self-conscious in his presence, but she wasn't sure why. Was it because they'd admitted an attraction to each other? Was it because they'd shared the most amazing first kiss she'd ever had? Was it because he'd asked her to get to know his daughter? Stephanie shook her head and turned away, calling over her shoulder, 'Well, I guess I'll see you at the hospital.'

'I guess you will. If I wait for you at the top of the street, will I be able to follow you?'

Stephanie turned back to face him and grinned. 'If you can keep up.'

'Think you're a Formula One driver, eh?'

Stephanie's answer was to laugh as she kept walking to her car. She felt bewildered, confused, excited and very happy. It was strange to feel such a wide range of emotions all at once, but she'd go with the flow and see where it took her.

She climbed behind the wheel of her car and started the engine. After buckling her seat belt, she reversed and drove around the block. There Oliver was, in a silver hire car, waiting at the top of the street. He indicated and pulled out behind her.

It wasn't as though the hospital was far—it probably would have taken them fifteen minutes to walk there—but the fact he thought he might get lost was kind of cute. Then again, as he'd driven to the house late at night in the fog, bone-weary from the incredibly hectic day he'd had, he had every right to claim disorientation, but she also knew after this one time of following her car to the hospital, he'd have his bearings and wouldn't need her help on that score again. Unless…

An impish smile crept across her face as she put her indicator on, taking him on a nice long detour around the back streets. She wondered if she could get away with crossing the main road as he would probably remember that was one of the things he hadn't had to contend with when he'd driven home.

A block away from the hospital, she decided she'd chance it. He was doing a good job of playing follow-the-leader and, while she knew they still had a stack of paper-work to get through at the office, surely another twenty minutes' delay couldn't hurt? He'd been rather stressed after Mrs Dixon's phone call so perhaps a bit of sightseeing would put him in a better mood to work with this morning. Besides, there was one sight in Katoomba *every* newcomer had to witness.

They were fortunate to get a green light and crossed the highway with little trouble. She checked in her rear-view mirror. Yes, he was still there. She slowed down, still obeying the speed limit, and headed towards the cliffs. The tourist buses had already arrived but they'd still be able to get a good look at Katoomba's most famous landmark.

Stephanie pulled into the car park and cut the engine, undoing her seat belt and climbing out before Oliver had finished parking. She locked her car and walked around to meet him. His look was one of feigned bewilderment as he followed suit and came to stand beside her.

'Funny. I don't remember the hospital grounds being this spacious yesterday. Then again, I didn't get to see all that much of them.'

Stephanie couldn't help the happiness she felt, glad he wasn't angry with her little detour. 'Come and see.' Eagerly, she took his hand in hers and led him down the path that led to the Three Sisters.

The three-rock formation rose steeply from the floor of the Jamieson Valley. The rocks' awesome beauty, their jagged sides, which had been weathered and eroded over the years, provided a breathtaking sight for locals and tourists.

Still holding his hand, Stephanie led him over to the rail and they looked out at the majestic view before them.

'The Aboriginal dream-time legend had it that three beautiful sisters fell in love with three brothers, but the brothers were from another tribe. Tribal law forbade them to marry but the brothers refused to accept this and decided to capture the three sisters. Well, this caused a tribal battle and the witchdoctor, fearing for the sisters' lives, changed them into stone to protect them. Alas, he was killed in the battle and there was no one else to reverse the spell.' She sighed romantically then shrugged. 'Personally, I just love coming here to marvel at the beauty of nature.' She pointed to the first 'sister'. 'You can actually walk out to the first one by going down those steps. Years ago, you could actually climb the other two, but they've stopped that due to erosion.'

Oliver surveyed the area around them and deep down inside Stephanie was desperate to see how he reacted. If he merely thought they were interesting and pretty to look at, then there would be no hope for any relationship between them. If, however, his soul was touched by their unsurpassed beauty, intrigued by their formation, and he could just sit there for hours looking at the valley below and cliffs on the opposite side, they would be well on their way to forming a deeper and lasting bond.

He gave her hand a little squeeze and pointed. 'Is that mist?'

She turned and looked to where he'd pointed, feeling the cool breeze on her face. 'Yes. Watch. Within a few minutes we'll be surrounded by whiteness and you won't be able to see anything.'

They stood, watching, their hands still linked, and just as Stephanie had said, soon they were caught up in a white cloud of swirling mists, the Sisters being obscured from view.

'I've never seen anything like it before. It's…majestic.'

Stephanie sighed with relief as he turned to face her.

'Thank you, Stephanie.' He bent and brushed his lips across hers and she gasped at the unexpected contact. 'Sorry. I didn't mean to startle you.'

'Startle away,' she flirted, and smiled up at him. He obliged but again only gave her lips a feather-light touch.

'You look lovely surrounded by white mist.'

She laughed. 'I suppose I stand out with my green hair and tinkling earrings.'

He joined in her laughter but turned and looked around him once more. 'I'll have to bring Kasey here. She's an outdoors person and would love the area.'

'What about Mrs Dixon?'

'Ooh, no,' he said in a silly high-pitched, well-modulated tone. 'Nature isn't for the likes of Mrs Dixon. She's better off staying warm inside with a nice cup of tea.'

Stephanie giggled. 'I'm sure you're wrong. The Blue Mountains have a way of luring a person outside to appreciate their beauty.'

'If you can coax Mrs Dixon out on an adventure, I'll…'
He paused, thinking what he'd do.

'You'll what?'

'Kiss you.'

'You've already done that.'

'Well, I'll have to do it again, then.'

'Is that so?' She raised her eyebrows. 'I thought you
wanted Mrs Dixon *in* the house to protect my virtue,' she
teased.

'That's not what I meant,' he countered. He breathed in
the fresh mountain air. 'Unfortunately, although I could
stay here all day and relax, I have a mountain of stress
waiting for me at the hospital. Now, if my guide would
stop playing "lose the tourist" games and actually take me
there, we might actually be able to get through some paperwork before she rushes off to her feeding frenzy.'

Stephanie laughed again, trying to figure out how he
could make her so happy when she hardly knew him. 'You
have a point. Not about the feeding frenzy, but the rest of
it.' They turned and walked back to the cars, still holding
hands.

'Shake your head so I can hear where you are,' Oliver
teased.

'The mist's not that thick.'

'I know, but I like the sound your earrings make.' Back
at the cars he reluctantly dropped her hand and fished his
keys from his pocket. 'So we're going to the hospital this
time?'

'I guess so,' she replied like a child who was being
forced to do something they didn't want to. 'You spoil all
my fun.' She unlocked her own car and climbed behind the
wheel. This time she behaved herself and within five
minutes they were driving into the hospital grounds. When
she'd climbed out, grabbing her bag and briefcase, she
smiled at him. 'See, I'm a woman of my word.'

'OK, woman of your word,' he said as they headed inside. 'Let's see how much paperwork we can get through in just over an hour.'

'You'd better let the triage sister know you're here first.'

'But of course.' They left their bags and coats in Oliver's office and headed for the A and E nurses' station.

'Ah, Oliver.' Jade picked up a sheaf of papers. 'These were delivered from Admin. Forms for hospital key-card, pagers, that sort of stuff.'

'Thank you. If you need me, I'll be in my office with Stephanie, trying to get through more of this *stuff*.' He waved the papers around and grimaced. Stephanie directed them to the tearoom and after they'd both sipped thankfully at their coffee-cups they settled down to work, sitting on opposite sides of the desk.

'I started making a list of the things you'd need to address first,' she said, reaching across the desk for a piece of paper buried beneath the in-tray. 'It was here yesterday morning,' she grumbled as she shifted things around.

'Leave it.' Oliver's tone was gruff and Stephanie glanced up at him, her hands still busy. They instantly stilled when she saw his gaze flick from her top to briefly meet her eyes before he looked away. 'I'll find it.'

She glanced down at her top and realised that from where he was sitting and from the way she was leaning he could see down her shirt. 'Oops.' She quickly settled back into the chair, adjusting her top, trying not to blush. She felt as though he'd actually caressed her and was surprised to find she liked it. Then again, after the kiss they'd shared that morning...why was she so surprised?

Oliver cleared his throat, his hands busy. 'Let's leave the list for now and just work with what's here.' He picked up a piece of paper and the awkward moment passed. Twenty minutes later, he picked up another manilla folder. 'Ah, rosters.'

'Ah, yes. The rosters. I'm sure that was on the top of my list for you to do.' She grinned. Everyone in the hospital knew how she loathed doing the rosters, always having to change things and juggle to suit people as best she could.

'Who's been drawing them up?'

'I have.'

He nodded as he scanned the contents. 'OK. Let's leave it that way.'

Stephanie froze, unable to believe what he'd just said. 'I'm sorry, did you say we'd leave it that way?'

'The arrangement? Yes. You know the staff, you're obviously used to doing them and that will be one less thing I have to worry about.'

'Ah... No!' she said in a sing-song voice laced heavily with determination.

'No?'

'No. Definitely not. I am *not* doing the rosters. I despise them—with a passion.'

'But I'm your boss.'

'So?'

'So I'm telling you it's your job to do them.'

'Telling me?'

'Yes. That's what bosses do. They tell their staff what to do.'

'Well, not this time.'

'They're just rosters, Steph.' He grinned, enjoying the sparks glowing in her eyes. She was stunning when she was angry.

'If that's all they are to you, then you do them.'

'But as the *assistant* director of A and E, it's your responsibility to...*assist* me.'

'I'll *assist* in any other way *except* to do the rosters.'

'Really? That's interesting. And if I make you?' His smile was increasing and although Stephanie knew he was winding her up, she couldn't help but respond.

'I'll quit.'

'You'll quit!' His tone was incredulous. 'That's a little drastic, isn't it?'

'Drastic times call for drastic measures.'

'Hmm.' Looking thoughtful, he steepled his fingers together. 'The rosters go for a month, right?'

'Yes.'

'If, before the next roster is due out, you can get Mrs Dixon to go on an adventure outdoors, I will take over doing the rosters.'

Stephanie raised her eyebrows in amazement. 'You want to bet on this?'

'Why not?'

'Because you're going to do them regardless.'

He shrugged acceptingly as though he hardly cared one way or the other. 'This way is more fun. Besides, are you saying you *couldn't* coax Mrs Dixon out for an adventure?'

'All right, then.' She held out her hand to his. 'You're on.'

He clasped her hand, shook it but then didn't let go. 'Are you sure about this?'

She met his gaze. 'Absolutely.'

'All right.' Slowly he released his hold, his fingers trailing lightly over her palm causing goose-bumps to sprinkle down her spine.

'OK.' She jerked her arm back as though burnt and cleared her throat. 'What's next?'

They managed to get through two more files before Oliver closed the last one he'd been looking at in disgust. 'Who set up the A and E structure here? It's a shambles.'

Stephanie was surprised at his vehemence. 'No, it's not. It works fine.'

'No, it doesn't. There is a more efficient and productive way to run this department than the way it's being run now.'

'You did mention yesterday that you were planning to make changes.'

'Correct.'

'Let me just caution you not to move too fast. This isn't some big city hospital where protocols are changed weekly. People here are used to doing things one way and one way only.'

'Then they're going to have to get used to doing things differently because the differences I intend to employ will bring about better working conditions and better time-management strategies, and those two combined will bring about happier and more productive workers.'

'I suppose you changed the way things were done at your last hospital?'

'Yes. If something works well, why not implement it? I believe in transformational leadership.'

'What?' Stephanie was amazed to find him so worked up and passionate about this. Still, she felt as though he'd waltzed into the hospital, taken a brief look around and was now trying to put his stamp on things as quickly as possible. Perhaps that was part of his contract? Perhaps it was part of the reason he'd been hired? It was no secret that she'd applied for the job of Director and, apart from the rosters, she'd have loved doing it, but she wouldn't have been changing things, especially not immediately after taking over the appointment.

'It's the process of cultural and philosophical change. Right now, those patients who come to A and E and are not priority-one cases can spend hours in the waiting room. Implementing my new strategies will change that. Time management is a huge issue affecting hospitals all over the world, and if this new model of management works, why not use it?'

'Who developed it?' Her arms were crossed defensively

Oliver straightened his shoulders and met her gaze fair and square. 'I did.'

She nodded slowly. 'So you intend to change things right now?'

'Why not? The sooner staff get used to the new regime *and* see for themselves how it works, the better this department will be.'

'So you're the knight in shining armour, riding in here to save us all from mismanagement.'

'Something like that, yes.'

She glanced at the clock behind him and quickly stood up. 'I need to go.'

'Of course.' He noticed the way her gaze didn't linger on him as it had earlier on. Instead, she stood, shrugged into her coat, wrapped her scarf around her neck and picked up her bag and briefcase.

'Do you need me to come back afterwards or can you *restructure* by yourself?'

'You're mad about this,' he stated.

'I'm annoyed you're jumping in straight away and not giving yourself time to settle in and at least get to know the staff. People don't take to change very well.'

'They never do. Even in big city hospitals, Stephanie.'

She walked to the door, a frown still on her face.

'If you wouldn't mind coming back, I could still do with your help.'

'Ha,' was all she said before she walked out, closing the door firmly behind her.

Oliver closed his eyes for a moment. He was weary and although he was looking forward to seeing Kasey tomorrow, he wasn't looking forward to the inner turmoil his recent visits with his daughter had brought. The sooner he began implementing changes at work, the sooner they'd be functioning the way they should and the sooner he could give Kasey more of his time.

One thing he had to do today was to convince Stephanie he was right. She was his ticket to the rest of the staff accepting the changes and he needed her on side.

CHAPTER SIX

STEPHANIE pulled her car into her brother's driveway and couldn't resist the urge to slam the door after she'd climbed out. She locked the car and stormed up to knock on Stephen's door, but he opened it before she could get that far.

'What's the matter?' He was dressed in his old painting clothes.

'Ooh, that man.' Stephanie walked past him, through the house, straight through to the lounge room, where she slumped onto one of the sofas.

'At least I know you're not talking about me.' He sat down next to her and waited. Stephanie took his hand in hers.

'You're so good to me. I'm so glad you're finally here.'

'Steph? You're starting to scare me. Whenever you get all mushy like this it means something's not going your way.'

'It's *him*.' She let go of his hand and pushed away, standing to pace the room.

Stephen thought for a moment before nodding. 'The new director. What's his name?'

'Oliver. Oliver Bowan.'

'Right. The one all the nurses were drooling over yesterday at Emergency.'

'Were they drooling?' Stephanie looked bothered.

'Even Nicolette thought he was good-looking.'

'Oh?' She changed tack and grinned at her brother. 'You don't look as though you enjoyed that revelation. Does it bother you that Nic might fancy someone besides you?'

She knew her words were making him uncomfortable and was glad to have a break from her own emotions even for just a few minutes. 'Last I saw, you were taking her home earlier this morning.'

'Hmm.' Stephen stood and walked out of the room. She followed him into the 1970s décor kitchen, glad to see he'd started removing the orange, brown and purple swirling wallpaper. 'Croissant and coffee to start with?' He took two cups from the cupboard.

'Answer the question, Stephen.'

'What question is that, Stephanie? You haven't asked me one.'

'Not verbally.' She grinned. 'How do you feel about Nic?'

'I hardly know her.' He poured coffee. 'Besides, we're soon to be professional colleagues so you'll just have to content yourself with the two of us being friends.'

Stephanie laughed at the idea. 'Friends? Yeah, right.' She leant forward and kissed him on the cheek. 'If you're waiting for my blessing, you have it. I can't think of anyone else who is more perfect for you than Nic.'

'Steph,' he growled.

'If, however, you need to delude yourself for a bit longer, then that's fine, too.'

'Steph!'

This time she acknowledged his warning tone. 'OK. Just don't leave it too long. She's a beautiful woman and some other man might snap her up.'

'Stephanie!'

'All right, all right. We won't talk about it any more.'

'Thank you.' He shook his head and smiled at her. 'Now it's my turn to grill you. Why does Oliver Bowan have your knickers in a knot?'

'He doesn't.' She accepted the coffee and sat down at his kitchen table. 'My knickers are perfectly fine.'

'Glad to hear it. Then why does he make you so mad?'

'He wants to change everything.'

'At the hospital?'

'Yes.'

Stephen nodded. 'His prerogative.'

'Today? Does he need to change things today? The man wasn't supposed to start until Saturday, but as he's now here he wants to get down and restructure the entire department.'

'Why does that bother you so much?'

'It doesn't bother me.'

'Sure, Steph.' He didn't believe her. 'Why does it bother you so much and does it have anything to do with the happy sensations I was experiencing a few hours ago?'

Stephanie put her coffee-cup on the table. 'He kind of kissed me.'

'But you hardly know him.'

'That's not all. He's staying in Gregor's house.'

'What? With you? Why?'

She explained about the estate agent mix-up. 'And that's not all.' She grimaced, knowing how her over-protective brother was going to take the news about Oliver's daughter. As she expected, Stephen hit the roof.

'You can move back in here. We'll drive round now and get your stuff.'

'No. It's fine.'

'It's not fine.'

She stood and placed a hand on his arm. 'It *is* fine. I'm fine. Although he makes me a little frustrated at times, I kind of, well…I kind of like him.'

'You kind of like him. He kind of kissed you and he kind of has a daughter. Is he really divorced? Can you trust anything this man says?'

She shook her head. 'I'm not going to discuss this with you any further. I'm not moving back here because you have your own life going on and I'm not going to cramp your style.'

'There's nothing to cramp. I've already told you, Nicolette and I are just friends.'

'Right. Forgive me for not believing you.' She reached for a croissant and pulled it apart. Thankfully, Stephen sat back down and watched her for a moment before following suit.

'I'm sorry,' he said eventually. 'I didn't mean to jump down your throat.' He raked a hand through his hair. 'I just know how hard it's been for you to have relationships, especially during the past year with me overseas.'

'And now you're here and you know how much I value your opinion.'

'So you don't mind if I check this Oliver guy out?'

She laughed, feeling better. 'Just be subtle…well, try at least.' She took a sip of her coffee. 'I know the man I eventually marry must understand the relationship we have, and I know that's partly the reason none of my previous boyfriends went the distance. Besides, with you not being around last year, it made it impossible for me to get a second opinion.'

'And now I'm here you feel as though you can take a chance?'

'If it ends in disaster you'll pick up the pieces and help me get back on my feet again. After all, that's what brothers are for.'

'You're not the most experienced person when it comes to relationships, Steph, and I mean that in the most wonderful way. You're so giving and accepting and that's when you end up getting hurt.'

'You think that because Oliver's not only been married but has a child he's going to run rings around me?'

Stephen nodded. 'He has experience in relationships that you don't.' He took her hand in his. 'You really like him?'

'I do.' She gazed at her brother. 'We have this...
connection.'

'When I saw you at the accident site, you didn't seem
too impressed with him.'

Stephanie couldn't help the smile that spread over her
lips. 'Oliver thought you and I were dating. He became a
little curt with me.'

'He was jealous? But he hardly knows you.'

Stephanie laughed and kissed her brother's cheek. 'Oh,
I've missed you so much. Now, are you going to feed me,
or are you going to feed me?'

Stephanie was on her way back to the hospital, her stomach
full of food, when her cellphone rang.

'Stephanie, where are you?'

'Oliver?'

'Who else would it be?'

'Plenty of people,' she countered as she pulled her car
to the side of the road so she could talk. 'What's up?'

'We've just had a call come in and I need you to go out
on retrieval.'

'There's no one else?'

'Meaning?'

'Well, it's my day off so I'm kind of low down on the
list to be called in.'

'I wouldn't have called you if I didn't need you.' His
voice had that haughtiness in it and she instantly knew he
was annoyed. It surprised her how well she knew him so
quickly. 'Where are you?'

She sighed, resigning herself to a 'Clayton's' day off—
the day off you had when you weren't having a day off!
'I'm ten minutes from the hospital.'

'Just get here,' he barked, and disconnected the call. It
seemed the ogre from last night was back, and this time he
didn't have the excuse of being misinformed.

When she arrived at the hospital, she parked her car and headed for his office. No sign of him. She went to A and E but still couldn't find him. She bumped into Jade. 'Have you seen Oliver?'

'He's in the tearoom, waiting for you, so he can start briefing everyone.'

'Thanks.' Stephanie grimaced and rushed to the tearoom, not wanting to hold things up any longer.

'Ah, Dr Brooks. Glad you could join us. Now we can begin. Two bush walkers have become lost in the mist around Jamieson Valley. Not only that, they took a wrong turn and ended up on the Golden Path, which is apparently closed. Now, you would think that would be enough for our intrepid explorers but, no, they wanted more excitement. They decided to climb their way up the closed path, and when the mist rolled in one of them slid, causing the other to follow, and both are now badly hurt. The reason we know all this is that they've dialled 112 on their cellphone and contacted emergency services. The call came through approximately ten minutes ago.

'David from police rescue will be co-ordinating the search and needs the medical team in place and ready for action.' Oliver consulted a sheet of paper. 'Arnold?'

'Yes.'

Oliver looked at the man who had answered. 'You'll be on point. You'll be liaising directly with the police rescue squad, as well as managing the whereabouts of our people.'

'Hey, tell me something I don't know,' Arnold teased, and people smiled. 'I'm the point guy and I'm good at it,' he said in his best Dirty Harry voice. Stephanie risked a glance at Oliver to see how he'd taken this answer to his instructions and was surprised to find him smiling as well. She released an unsteady breath, glad he'd been able to find his sense of humour.

'OK.' He handed out a few more jobs, people nodding

and asking a few questions to make sure they knew exactly where they were needed. 'Stephanie, you'll be with me.'

'Ooh,' Arnold said, and made a few kissy noises. Stephanie could feel her face beginning to grow hot. She was used to Arnold's teasing and should have half expected it, but again was concerned how Oliver might take it.

'Oh, keep quiet,' Oliver told him, his smile still in place. 'You're just jealous because she doesn't get to stay with you.'

'You've got that straight,' Arnold replied, and winked at Steph.

'All right, people. Let's get moving. The ambulance leaves in ten minutes.' As people bustled out of the room, Oliver's gaze met Stephanie's. 'Got a second?'

'Only one. The ambulance leaves in ten minutes.'

He came and stood beside her, straightening the papers he held in his hand. 'How was brunch?'

'Good.' She glanced down at the paper and noticed he had the preplanned lists she'd written regarding allocation of staff for emergency procedures. 'I see you've been working hard.' She motioned to the notes.

'Yes. In fact, I'd just finished browsing through them when the call came through, so they've been very helpful.'

'We'd better get moving if we're going to make that ambulance,' she said.

'I know. Listen, the reason I wanted you with me was because—'

'I'm a brilliant doctor. I know.'

'No, seriously…'

'Oliver, you don't need to explain.'

'I just don't want you or the rest of the staff thinking I'm playing favourites.'

'You mean you're not?' she replied, feigning surprise. That small, sweet grin she was beginning to love spread across his lips.

'It's just I mentioned to Lauren this morning about our accommodation mix-up—as you suggested we should—and she told me she was surprised a girl like you was my type. Now, I have no idea what that means, neither do I care, but I wanted to give you a heads-up that the grapevine rumours have already started.'

Stephanie tried not to wince at the label. *A girl like her.* Terrific. She filed it away. Now was not the time. 'Hence Arnold's reaction?'

'Exactly.'

'OK.' She shrugged. 'Thanks.' She headed out of the room, forcing her mind to focus on the tasks ahead.

She was one of the last to get into the ambulance, her bright orange retrieval suit matching those of her colleagues, and, as she had yesterday, she chose the transport Oliver wasn't in. Yesterday she'd chosen it because she'd wanted the distance from him. Today she needed everyone to see that they were just colleagues, nothing more. But *you are something more*, the little voice inside her head said, and she frowned, brushing it away.

'So…' Kevin, the paramedic, said. 'I hear you and Oliver are sharing a place.'

Stephanie smiled, knowing the rest of the staff who were travelling with them were almost holding their breath with excited anticipation to hear what she was going to say. 'Yes. It's only for a few weeks until he finds permanent accommodation. In fact, his daughter arrives tomorrow, along with the housekeeper-cum-nanny. I'll either be hibernating in my room or doing double shifts at the hospital.'

'Sounds like a plan,' Kevin remarked, and after that, nothing else was said. Discussion turned to the possible scenarios they might find. Stephanie was pleased with the information she'd managed to relay and was proud of the way she'd done it—without letting the rest of her colleagues see exactly how much their new boss *really* affected her.

When they arrived, David had a headset on and was speaking rapidly to one of his staff. He motioned for Stephanie to come over and, without saying a word, held out an abseiling harness to her. She immediately put it on.

'Going somewhere?' Oliver asked as he sauntered over. David spoke intently to his staff member and held out a harness to Oliver as well.

'Looks like, wherever it is I'm going, you're coming, too, boss.'

'Looks that way.'

'Right.' David turned his attention to them. 'The bush walkers have been located. Nothing too life-threatening, from what my people can see, although if they stay down there much longer, they run the risk of hypothermia.'

'Stabilise and evacuate?'

'Got it in one. I thought we might need a few extra of your people to go down but the two of you will be sufficient. Once you're down, let Arnold know what you need, he'll get it together and we'll get it down for you. Getting them out is going to be a different matter. We're going to need to venture a few kilometres back the way they walked this morning before we can hook up the ropes to get them out. The tree foliage is too dense here.'

'OK,' Stephanie said as David put a hard hat on her head, making her earrings tinkle. 'What's the best way to get down?'

'There's a disused walking path over there. That'll take you about half of the way, and from there we've rigged up a rope you can hold on to while you navigate to the bottom. They're not far from there.'

He handed Oliver a walkie-talkie. 'Give us a shout if you run into trouble.'

Oliver tucked the communication device into a pocket in

the retrieval overalls. 'Let's grab the emergency medi-kits from Arnold then we're ready.'

It was another five minutes before they set off, the medi-kits secure inside their overalls to ensure their hands were free.

'Ready to rock 'n roll?'

Oliver smiled. 'Ladies first.'

After receiving David's blessing they headed off. As they descended, Stephanie pulled on her pair of heavy-duty gloves so she was ready when they came to the next section.

'So, is your brother doing anything that's going to hinder the rescue operation today? He's not trapped somewhere? Playing with matches? Nothing like that?'

'I don't know. I don't think so or, should I say, I don't *feel* so.'

'Thank goodness for that.' The path was becoming a little steeper now and when David had said it was disused, he'd meant overgrown. Glad of the heavy-duty overalls, Oliver pulled on his gloves to help fend off the coarse bushes and not risk cutting his hands. 'So, tell me, what did Lauren mean when she said "a girl like you"? It has me intrigued.'

'I thought it didn't bother you.'

'It doesn't. It's just something I'd like clarified and, besides, we have the time.'

'Perfect climbing-down-the-hill conversation, eh?'

'Something like that.'

Stephanie concentrated on where she was putting her feet, and as she was in front she was also trying to make sure she didn't accidentally whack Oliver with the branches she was holding back to clear the path. 'The phrase, "a girl like you" can have so many different connotations.'

'Exactly, which is why I'm asking.'

'Well, let's break it down a little. Lauren is a very good nurse but a determined flirt.'

'Agreed. I've hardly set foot in the place and she's already asked me out.'

'Is that why you told her about our…living arrangements?'

'She was inviting herself around for dinner tonight. She wanted to cook for me.' His tone was incredulous and then he shuddered. 'As I said, she's from the same mould as my ex-wife, and I'm definitely not going down that track again.'

'OK. So if Lauren is a flirt, what do you think *she* would mean by her comment?'

'Someone different to her?'

'Exactly.'

'But I already knew that.' Oliver groaned as though disappointed he hadn't found out any new information.

'Look, there's the rope. Thank goodness. How David calls this a path is beyond me.'

'Do you know how to hook the harness to the rope?'

'Yes. Do you?'

'Yes.'

'Hmm. A man of hidden talents, eh?'

'A woman of hidden talents. Hey, is that what Lauren meant?'

'Oh, give it a rest.'

'Tell me what she really meant and stop avoiding the issue.'

Stephanie had hooked herself to the rope and held it firmly in position as she turned her back on the steeper part of the mountain, preparing to go down. 'In Lauren's world, the phrase means I haven't had much experience with men.'

'Really?' His eyebrows were raised in surprise and, without wanting to say any more, Stephanie began her descent. She heard Oliver call in on the walkie-talkie that they were at the rope and heading down. She presumed one of David's men would be at the base, waiting for them.

When the sections allowed, she gave a few little jumps covering more distance, but for the most part, the area was quite dense and therefore required all her concentration.

Sure enough, when she reached the ground, one of David's men, Billy, was there to greet her. 'Hi, Steph,' he said. 'Where's your partner in crime?'

'On his way.'

'Good. Once he's down they'll be sending the stretchers down via pulley so I need to re-rig this rope.'

'He shouldn't be far.'

He wasn't. Oliver touched down and unhooked his rope.

'I'll let David know you're down,' Billy said. 'Walk about two hundred metres along the path in that direction…' he pointed '…and you can't miss them. Two of our staff are keeping the patients company.'

'Thanks, Billy.'

As they headed off, Oliver walked behind her. 'So what does that mean?'

'What?' she asked as she pulled off her gloves and stowed them in a pocket.

'That you haven't had much experience with men.' Oliver followed suit with his own gloves.

'It means just that.'

'You've never had a broken engagement? Steady boyfriend for years and years?'

'Nope. I've had a few boyfriends—all one at a time,' she added with an impish grin.

'Good. Good to hear that.'

'But none of them stuck.'

'Stuck?'

'You know, gelled.'

'Why? Are you too picky? Too fussy?'

'You'd better believe it. No second best for me.'

'Is that a warning?'

Stephanie merely smiled. 'Besides, if I feel like hanging out with a man, I have Stephen, remember.'

'That's right. The twin brother. I guess any man worthy of you must first receive your brother's blessing?'

'Of course. What about you? Do you have any siblings?'

'Yes. I have one brother. We don't talk, are completely opposite, so naturally we have nothing in common.' He paused. 'Well, maybe, except for Nadele.'

'Your ex-wife?'

'She told me the day before I left to come to Australia that she was seeing Augustus.'

'I presume that's your brother. Does that bother you?'

'No. In fact, they're perfect for each other. You see, Augustus doesn't like children, can't tolerate them.'

'Ah. So if Nadele gets together with Augustus, you have a better chance of getting Kasey away from her mother's influence?'

'Wow. You're not just a pretty face, Dr Brooks.'

Stephanie turned and smiled at him. 'Why, thank you.' As she wasn't looking where she was going, she stumbled and Oliver quickly put out a hand to stop her from falling. They both stopped, their bodies close, their breaths mingling. The contact was sudden and unexpected, yet both of them reacted as though they'd been starving for it. The moment continued to hold as they gazed into each other's eyes. The timely hissing from the walkie-talkie brought them both back to reality with a thud.

'Hmm.' Oliver frowned as they started off again, pulling the radio from his pocket and answering David's call. 'We should be almost there,' he said. 'Is there a problem?'

'One of the patients has lost consciousness.'

'OK. The path isn't too bad here so we'll step it up.'

'Safety first,' David reminded him.

They picked up the pace and continued along the path,

glad when it became wide enough for them to walk side by side. Stephanie had been conscious of Oliver walking behind her and although she knew the orange retrieval suit wasn't very flattering, she couldn't help feeling his gaze roving over her from time to time.

Finally they heard the police rescue staff in the distance and both pulled out their medi-kits ready for action.

'I'll take the unconscious patient, you do triage on the other one.'

'Understood.' Stephanie had her medi-kit open so the instant she knelt by her patient she was able to pull on a pair of gloves. 'Hi, I'm Stephanie.'

'Inga.'

'Where does it hurt?'

'My arm, my leg. I think I twisted my ankle. Is Utta all right?' She gestured to her friend.

'He's being looked after.' Stephanie felt Inga's ankle and wasn't surprised when her patient gave a yelp of pain. 'Anywhere else?'

'No, but I feel sore everywhere. My backside hurts.'

'OK.' Stephanie picked up the medical torch and checked Inga's eyes, but both pupils were reacting normally. Next, she unfolded the cervical collar from the kit and placed it around Inga's neck. 'How about your head? Does it hurt anywhere?'

'I think I bumped it.'

'Where?'

Inga showed her the spot and although Stephanie could feel a lump forming, there was no blood.

'Steph,' came Oliver's call.

'I'll be back in a moment, Inga.' Stephanie stood and walked the few steps to where Oliver was tending to Utta. She knelt down.

'His left arm feels broken and he has a possible dislocated shoulder.'

'That's probably what took the brunt of the fall.'

'Left pupil is a little sluggish and there's a crack at the base of his skull.'

Stephanie checked Utta's pupils. 'Probably what's caused the loss of consciousness. Utta?' she called. 'Utta, can you hear me?' She took the pulse in his fractured arm, making sure there was still a steady flow of blood. It was weak but it was there. Carotid pulse was a little stronger, which gave them both a positive indication.

'Utta?' Inga said, but Stephanie blocked out the other woman's panicked calls.

'We'll need to get him out a.s.a.p. Do you have a sphygmo in your kit?'

'No. Want me to get Arnold to send one down?'

'Yes. Utta's going to go into shock if we're not careful.'

'Give me the walkie-talkie.' Stephanie took the radio from him and called up their request. 'You think he's going to be stable enough to move?'

'I want his BP checked before I make that call.'

'Right. I'll give Inga pain meds so I can splint her ankle, then at least she'll be ready for transfer.' She returned her attention to Inga. 'Are you allergic to any medications?'

'Utta? How's Utta?'

'Utta is unconscious at the moment, Inga. He hit his head a bit harder than you did. We're monitoring him as best we can and hopefully soon we'll have you both out of here.' Once they'd arrived, both police rescue men had gone to do the next part of their job—one to help with the stretchers and the other to prepare the area from where the stretchers would be winched to the top.

'I want to give you something to take away the pain, but I need to know if you're allergic to anything.'

'No. Not that I know of.'

'Have you had morphine before?'

'Yes.'

'Good.' Stephanie drew up the injection and administered it. 'That should help.' She checked Inga's eyes and pulse again. 'Good,' she repeated. 'OK. We'll just let the morphine take effect.'

She turned to Oliver who had just finished bandaging Utta's head. 'Bleeding under control?'

'Yes. Left pupil still a little sluggish. Right one is fine.'

'Pulses?'

'No change.'

Stephanie returned her attention to splinting Inga's ankle and once she'd finished, they heard the sounds of people heading in their direction. 'Hallelujah,' she said as a larger emergency medi-kit was carried into view by one of their police rescue colleagues.

Stephanie took Utta's BP with the sphygmomanometer. 'We need to move him, now. Get the stretcher.'

Working together as a team, they successfully transferred Utta to the stretcher, all of them rather pleased when their patient groaned in pain. 'Hello, there,' Oliver said with a smile. 'Utta? Can you hear me?'

Another groan. 'Good. We're about to take you out of here so hang in. Steph, you stay with Inga and I'll head up with Utta.' Their gazes locked for a moment and both acknowledged the growing awareness between them, but then Oliver smiled and said a little more tenderly, 'See you up top and remember—be safe.'

She returned his smile. 'Yes, boss.'

'The other stretcher was on its way down when we left to bring this one here, so Billy and Krystal should be along with it in another five minutes,' her colleague said.

'Great. Thanks.' Stephanie watched them head off before taking Inga's vitals again, glad to have the sphygmo to check her patient's blood pressure. 'How are you feeling?'

'Foolish.' Tears glistened in Inga's eyes and she shut them tight.

'Hey. You'll both be fine.'

'The mist just came from nowhere.'

'It does that and has caught many an unsuspecting tourist unawares. Are you in any pain?'

'No.'

'Good. Shouldn't be too much longer and you'll be following Utta out of here.'

Inga sniffed. 'He will be all right, won't he?'

'He's regained consciousness so that's a good sign.' At this information Inga seemed to relax and, thankfully, Billy and Krystal appeared soon after. 'All right, Inga, let's get you organised and on your way out of here.' Stephanie checked her patient's vital signs before they moved her, and when she was settled and all the equipment had been accounted for and packed away, they headed off to the extraction point.

As they walked along, they encountered more mist and Stephanie was grateful for the helmet on her head, complete with light. She followed Billy, with Krystal bringing up the rear, and when they stopped for a break she checked Inga again, wrapping the space blanket more securely around her. 'The last thing we want is you getting cold,' she told Inga with a smile. 'Not much longer and we'll have you out of here.'

Unfortunately, it was a bit longer than anticipated as they needed to wait for the mist to thin a little before they could winch the stretcher out. Utta's stretcher had made it to the top just after the mist had rolled in.

Oliver was still at the bottom, having let the police rescue staff escort the stretcher up. 'They know more about that than I do, and Utta was as stable as I could get him,' he told Stephanie as they sat down to wait.

Finally the call came down to say they were ready to begin, and Billy and Krystal escorted the stretcher up.

'It won't be long.' Billy grinned at them as the winches started. 'I promise we won't forget you.'

'You'd better not, Billy. I know where you live, remember,' Stephanie retorted good-naturedly, and although she wouldn't admit it to any of her colleagues, she was more than happy to be left alone with Oliver.

When the rescue party was out of sight and the natural sounds around them returned, they resumed their waiting positions, Stephanie sitting on a small rock opposite Oliver.

'You know, annoying as it is that we can't move, it's really very pretty here.' He looked around him at the slowly lifting mist.

Stephanie was happy he seemed to find an affinity with this place, with these mountains. 'When you lived in Sydney, did you come up here much?'

'I remember coming up here on a school excursion and I'm pretty sure we visited the Three Sisters, but about the only thing I can recall about that trip was that the girls' school came along, too.'

Stephanie smiled. 'Chasing girls rather than looking at the sights?'

'Something like that.' Oliver's gaze filtered with hers. 'Now, though, I'm more than happy to do both. Chase the girl *and* look at the sights.'

Stephanie's smile slowly disappeared and her lips parted. His gaze said he liked looking at her, even though she was dressed in an orange suit. Her heart rate increased and she marvelled at the way she was a sucker for his smooth-talking lines.

'Well, if you said things like that and looked at the girls back then the way you're looking at me, it's no wonder you remember little about that trip.'

His face was serious as he said, 'I'm not feeding you lines, Steph. I'm a good twenty-odd years older than the boy who was here all that time ago. How can you doubt that I find you attractive? That I think you're not only intelligent but beautiful as well?'

A nervous laugh escaped her lips. 'In an orange suit and green hair. Don't you think they clash?'

'On some people maybe, but not you. You carry it off with finesse.'

'It's so easy to believe everything you say while we're down here, in this little bubble of white, but don't forget I'm still a girl with little dating experience.'

'I think you do yourself a great injustice. It's not the amount of experience I care about but how sincere you are, and perhaps that's one of the things which makes you unique from the Laurens of this world. You are sincere and in my life that's been a rare commodity and is something I value highly when I find it.'

He didn't move from where he was sitting but somehow she found herself beside him, unaware she'd moved. He didn't speak, he didn't make a move to touch her. Instead, he merely looked at her and she at him.

'I'm scared of you,' she whispered.

'Surely you don't mean that.'

'I'm scared of how you make me feel and the fact that I don't even know you. You've been in my life less than forty-eight hours—'

'And yet the time we've spent together has been intense and riddled with emotions.'

'Yes. See? You seem to know me so well.'

'That's because I do. It's as though I've been waiting for you all my life.' As soon as he said the words, he shook his head and groaned. 'I can't believe I just said that.'

Stephanie smiled, feeling her earlier apprehension float away with the mist. 'Pretty corny, Dr Bowan.'

'Yes, but nevertheless it's the truth. As is the fact that I want to kiss you again.'

She felt a wave of pleasure spread over her at his words,

warming her through and through. 'When you say things like that, I find it hard to breathe.'

He nodded, still not making a move. 'Hyperventilation isn't good, Dr Brooks.'

She kept wondering why he didn't make any effort to touch her. He was saying all the right things but not following through on them. Then it dawned on her. He wanted her to make the move, to let him know this really was what she wanted. She'd met him head on that morning but, still, he'd initiated the kiss. Now it was her turn, but she'd always let the man lead before.

'Oliver.' She reached and caressed his rough cheek with her fingertips. 'I feel so vulnerable.'

'So do I.'

'I don't know if this is a good idea or not.'

'Neither do I.'

Her tongue came out to wet her lips and his gaze eagerly followed the action. Drawing on the yearning that seemed to have tripled in an instant, she leaned forward and pressed her lips to his.

CHAPTER SEVEN

IT WAS as though a conspiracy was in place and any time he wanted to kiss this amazing woman, a buzzer or phone would go off. This time was no different, with the walkie-talkie choosing that moment to hiss with static as a message was relayed.

The noise startled Stephanie, causing her to jump, effectively breaking their kiss. Oliver stood and pulled out the radio as David spoke.

'The patients are on their way to the hospital and the winches are on their way down to you. Make sure all equipment is secure and harnessed to you.'

'Will do.'

'Call when you're ready to come up, and keep the channel open while you're on the winch.'

'Copy that.' Oliver replaced the walkie-talkie in his pocket and looked down at Steph. 'Interrupted again.' He smiled and shook his head. 'I can't seem to cut a break.'

She laughed, amazed at how comfortable she felt after such an intense moment. It was as though he knew she needed a sense of normalcy, and humour was good at providing that.

'When we get back to the hospital, please, go home and try and enjoy what's left of your day off. I know there's still heaps of paperwork to get through but I'll cope until tomorrow.'

'But what about Inga and Utta? You don't want me to follow through?'

He took her hand in his and squeezed. 'Enjoy the rest of

the day and relax. I'll be working you hard enough, and goodness knows when you'll get another day off.'

'Does this mean you're conceding? You'll do the rosters?'

'You have to win the bet first.'

'It's in the bag.'

'So confident but you forget, I know Mrs Dixon and you don't.'

'Ah, but I have an ace up my sleeve.'

'And what, pray, is that?' He stood there with his hands on his hips, very sure of himself, but there was no way Stephanie was going to lose this bet and she'd take every advantage she had. Standing on tiptoe, she quickly leaned in and kissed him before whispering against his mouth, 'I know the perfect place to take her. She won't be able to resist.'

'Well, I certainly can't,' he said, and captured her mouth with his, returning the favour of her surprise kiss.

The sound of the winch grew louder and Oliver groaned, breaking the contact. 'See? Something always interrupts us.'

Stephanie giggled, feeling happy.

Two hours later, when Oliver arrived at the house, Stephanie was sitting in her favourite wing-backed chair, the classical strains of Chopin filling the air.

He tossed his briefcase, coat and tie into his room and was undoing the top button of his shirt and rolling up his sleeves as he walked into the room. 'Relaxed?'

'I guess.'

He watched her for a second. 'You're knitting!'

'That's right. Well done.' She tugged at the wool, not missing a beat. 'You really are a smart man.'

'And Chopin? I'd pegged you as a heavy-rock type of girl.'

She shook her head, her earrings tinkling lightly. 'That's Stephen.'

'Really?' He seemed amazed.

'I'm a home body at heart.'

'Do your home skills lean towards cooking?' He sniffed the air appreciatively.

'Yes, as a matter of fact they do. I've made soup.'

'From scratch?'

'How else do you make it?'

He shrugged. 'I don't know. Open a can.'

'Please, tell me Mrs Dixon cooks or I'm not going to survive this experience.'

Oliver chuckled as he walked into the kitchen. 'Of course she cooks. Didn't I tell you she was our housekeeper for most of my childhood?'

'So? Keeping house and cooking are different things.'

'True.' He returned a moment later. 'Is that ready to eat?'

'Yes. Just let me finish off the row. There are some rolls warming in the oven.'

'I'll get it. You keep…knitting.' He smiled as he said the last word.

'What's wrong with me knitting?' she demanded.

'Nothing. At least it's colourful. That fits with the image have of you.' He walked off again. Once she'd finished he row, she went in search of him. 'What is it you're knitting? Not that I'm being offensive or criticising your talent. Just curious.'

'A scarf.' She settled herself on a bench stool and watched him.

'Very colourful scarf.'

'Yes. I'm making it as an engagement gift for Nic. It'll match the one I made for Stephen a while back.'

'Nicolette's getting engaged to Stephen?'

'She will be. Neither of them know it yet but it's a certainty.'

'How do you know?'

She shrugged. 'I'm his sister. She's my friend. I jus
know. Besides, she respects the bond Stephen and I share.

He nodded as he gathered soup bowls, plates, napkin
and spoons, setting everything up on the bench before dish
ing up. 'Smells wonderful.'

'Thank you.' She waited until he'd taken his first sip
before she took hers.

'Mmm. Tastes wonderful, too.'

'Thank you again. You are good for my ego, Dr Bowan.

'Does your ego need bolstering?'

'Doesn't everyone's?'

'Not necessarily. Lauren's certainly doesn't. That woma
has claws.'

'Still trying, is she?'

'She's certainly trying her best. I hope you don't mind
but I started a rumour that we're already dating.'

Stephanie's spoon clattered into her bowl. 'You di
what!' Her mouth hung open in stunned amazement.

'I'm joking.'

She dragged air into her lungs and the tension eased a
quickly as it had built.

He waited a few moments before saying, 'Is the ide
unpalatable to you?'

'You and I dating?'

He nodded.

'No,' she answered slowly. 'But I don't know if it's a
good idea.'

'Why not? The attraction's there.'

'That's just an attraction, Oliver. They have been know
to peter out before. Also, you have your daughter arriving
tomorrow and I'm no expert, but the last thing she'll need
while she's adjusting to a new country is a new woman in
her father's life.'

'I had thought of that.'

'How long is Kasey here for?'

'The summer. Well, the northern hemisphere summer.'

'Would you like her with you permanently?'

'That's my current plan.'

'If only Nadele would let go?'

'Exactly.'

'That's probably another reason why we shouldn't let anything develop between us. It may cause even more friction for you.'

Again, she had a point and it wasn't one he liked as he knew it was pretty accurate. Still, a part of him wanted to know. 'My ex-wife and daughter aside, do you find the prospect of dating me so…bad?'

Stephanie couldn't help but smile at him. 'Not…bad *per se*. I just don't think it's a good idea right now.'

'So where does that leave us?'

'Friends?'

Oliver nodded and ate another mouthful of soup. 'Friends.'

Yet the look they shared across the bench was a mutual acknowledgement that they were both fooling themselves.

The next morning, Stephanie woke to find a note from Oliver on the kitchen bench. 'Coffee's ready, eat healthy, see you at the hospital…*friend*.' He hadn't signed it but she still admired the bold strokes, glad to find a doctor whose writing was legible.

With a smile on her face and a spring in her step, she drank a cup of coffee, had a shower and ate a bowl of cereal before dressing and happily heading to work to see her *friend*. There would definitely be problems if they decided to pursue this attraction between them and she hoped they'd be able to control themselves, but the fact that he'd left her a note and the fact that she'd reacted the way she had made her wonder just how successful they would be.

When she opened the door to Oliver's office, he looked up from the papers in front of him.

'Finally.' There was no smile and her earlier warm fuzzies disappeared.

'Problem?'

He put his pen down and leaned back in the chair, stretching his arms above his head.

'Oh, don't lean back too far,' she cautioned, but she was too late as the chair began to tip backwards. The next thing she saw were Oliver's legs going up, his arms clutching helplessly at the air and a look of horror on his face. The crash came next as he ended up sprawled on the floor, his legs tangled with the chair.

'The chair's broken,' she finished lamely. 'Sorry. I should have mentioned that yesterday.' Trying not to laugh at the sight of him, she went around the desk to help him.

'You think?' he snapped sarcastically. 'And don't you dare laugh,' he added when he saw her twitching lips.

'I wouldn't dream of it,' she replied, not trying in the least to get rid of the smile. She held out her hand. 'Let me...'

'I'm fine,' Oliver muttered.

'Of course you are.' She stepped back. 'I'm surprised you haven't gone over before now but, rest assured, a new chair has been ordered. It's due on Friday, in time for the new director's arrival.'

'So I suppose this is all my fault for arriving early.' Stephanie's answer was to continue grinning at him as he stood and righted the chair. 'What would have happened if I'd been able to come a few weeks ago when my contract was officially due to begin?'

'It wasn't broken then.'

'How did it break? No,' he continued, holding up his hands. 'I don't want to know.' He sat back down.

'Can I get you a cup of coffee? Tea? Biscuits?'

'You can sit down and help me get through this paper-work.'

'Right you are, boss.' Stephanie did as she was told and picked up the piece of paper he'd been reading when she'd arrived. She frowned. 'This is a report on expenditure.'

'I can see that.'

'Good. Then we can move on.'

Oliver breathed in deeply and was once more treated to the mesmerising scent she wore. 'Vanilla.'

'Vanilla?' She glanced at the report and then her eyes widened as she realised what he meant. 'Oh. Sorry.' She dropped the report like a hot potato.

'Don't apologise. I guess it's just something we need to get used to.' He raked his hand through his hair. 'To work, Dr Brooks.'

'Good idea, Dr Bowan. Where do you want to start?'

'At the top and slowly work my way down.' His voice was husky and Stephanie's gaze darted to meet his, widening when she saw the obvious desire there. Her lips formed a little O and her breathing increased. He was glad the idea seemed to set her alight because the same idea had been setting him alight for most of the night. Once more he'd hardly slept because he'd been too busy thinking of the woman who was living under the same roof as him. What was it about her that made him unable to control himself? He'd never had this sort of trouble with a woman before. Usually, he pigeonholed his life into nice, neat compartments in his mind, taking them out only when he needed to address certain issues. With Stephanie, however, pigeonholing wasn't working. She kept staying where she was, in the centre of his thoughts, and it was starting to drive him crazy.

He cleared his throat and eventually broke his gaze from hers. 'Now it's my turn to apologise, even though what I said is true. We need to work, and first on the agenda is the new restructuring for A and E.'

Oliver shuffled some papers on the desk and found the sheet he was looking for. The sheet was covered with the same bold strokes as the note he'd left her that morning…the note she'd put in her top bedside drawer so she could read it over and over again like a silly schoolgirl in the throes of her first crush.

'OK. As you know, waiting times in A and E are usually astronomical if you're not an urgent case.' He waited for her nod before continuing. 'My restructuring protocol is to change the way the triage system operates. Instead of having the numbers from one to five, one being urgent, five being extremely non-urgent, the cases are split into surgical and medical.

'The triage sister can then decide which is the most urgent of each, but this way people are in and out of A and E a lot sooner. This will also cut down on the patients having several different staff members looking after their case due to shift changes. Naturally shift changes happen but the commonality of it would be reduced.'

'That would mean we need two shifts on at any given time.'

'That's right. One medical team and one surgical team for each shift.'

Stephanie rolled her eyes and leaned back in the chair, her arms crossed in front of her. 'You are definitely taking over the rosters. I'm not touching that one with a forty-foot pole. That would be a nightmare.'

'Actually, it isn't. Everyone still has the same number of shifts as they have now, but the shifts are restructured.' He went on to explain the finer details and as he spoke his words actually began to make sense. Stephanie was sure he was hypnotising her with his deep, rich tone. He had a voice she would never tire of hearing, it was so delicious. *He* was so delicious.

'So, what do you think?' Oliver looked at her, eagerly awaiting a response.

'You have a very sexy smile.'

'Stephanie!' He pushed the chair back and stood, shaking his head.

'OK. I think it has merit.'

'Really?'

She laughed. 'You're as excited as a kid in a candy store. Yes, I think it sounds good and the fact it's been trialled in other hospitals is certainly a good recommendation.'

Relief washed over him. 'Then you'll help me convince the rest of the staff?'

She raised her eyebrows. 'You planned it this way, didn't you?'

'I knew I'd need your help, yes.'

'Is this why you've made passes at me? To keep me on side?'

'Ha. I've been trying to keep you on side by *not* making passes.'

She gave him a wry grimace. 'Didn't work.'

'What? Getting you on side or not making passes?'

Stephanie smiled. 'The latter.'

'Seriously, will you help?'

'The rosters will be a nightmare, especially if people are rostered on for a whole week with someone they don't like.'

'I expect them to be professional about their work.'

'And they are.'

'But I understand your concern and am relying on you to make sure the teams don't have members who clash.'

'Fair enough.'

Oliver yawned.

'Didn't sleep well last night?'

'Not particularly.' He gave her a lopsided smile. 'I was plagued with thoughts about my assistant director.'

'Plagued?'

He merely grinned and smothered another yawn. His phone rang and he was glad of the interruption.

'Oliver, it's Sophie. We have two ambulances due in five minutes. MVA. Is Steph with you?'

'Yes. We'll be right there.' He hung up. 'Motor vehicle accident.'

'This early in the morning?'

'People rushing to work,' he said as she stood.

'Especially if they didn't get enough sleep last night,' she added as they headed out the door.

'Tired and rushing.'

'Recipe for disaster,' she finished.

He turned from locking his door to glare at her. 'I was just about to say that.' He closed his eyes for a brief second. 'Will you get out of my head?'

'Why? Does it disturb you?'

'Yes.'

She grinned. 'Good. That makes two of us.' With that, she headed off to A and E, leaving him to follow.

When Oliver had seen the estimated-injury report from the paramedics, he called in extra staff, including Stephen.

'I guess it's about time I got to know your brother,' he said softly as they stood at the nurses' station.

'Uh…why?' Stephanie was a little apprehensive. Hadn't they decided last night to be just friends? Although with all the flirting they'd done so far today, they weren't off to a very strong beginning.

'I'm sure you can figure it out.' He gave her a wink as Sophie walked up, cutting short any other questions she might ask.

'Both trauma rooms 1 and 2 are ready to go.'

'Thank you. Stephanie, you and Jade start in TR-1—

Sophie, you'll be with me. When Stephen arrives, get him to help out where necessary.' He picked up the paramedic report and studied it, silently shaking his head. 'These kids are six and eight. Who's the paediatrician on call?'

'Daisy Brambles,' Sophie supplied.

'Pardon?'

'That's her name.' Stephanie stood as the wail of ambulance sirens filled the air. 'Showtime.'

'Have Dr Brambles notified and here a.s.a.p.,' Oliver said as he followed Stephanie to the trauma rooms.

'What do we have?' Stephanie asked the paramedic as the first patient was wheeled into TR-1.

'Thirty-five-year-old woman, blunt-force trauma to the chest from steering-wheel, possible fractures to the right scapula and humerus, possible fractures to the right tibia and fibula, whiplash, lacerations and bruising.'

'No loss of consciousness?'

'No. Airway and circulation all functioning well, breathing a little raspy due to possible pneumothorax or fractured ribs.'

'Thanks.' Stephanie looked down at her patient who was strapped to the stretcher with a cervical collar, oxygen mask in place. 'Hello, I'm Stephanie. What's your name?' Her patient hesitated. 'It's OK. You can speak with the mask on.'

'Anita.'

'Can you tell me what happened?'

'I was turning the corner into the street a few blocks away from my kids' school and this other car just ploughed right into me.'

'Right, Anita. I'm just going to have a look at you. I know you've been given something mild for the pain but is there anywhere that's really sore?' Stephanie checked Anita's pupils, glad they were contracting normally.

'No. My arm was really sore before but it's not too bad now. My kids? Are they OK?'

'They're being taken care of.' Next Stephanie hooked her stethoscope into her ears and listened to Anita's chest. 'How's your breathing? Does it hurt to breathe?'

'A little.'

Stephanie nodded and listened closely. 'There's a slight hyper-resonance but other than that it's not too bad. ECG, thanks, Jade. Anita, have you had a chest X-ray before?'

'Yes. Quite a few years ago.'

'Good.'

Jade gave her report of Anita's BP, temp and respiratory rates, all of which were noted in Anita's file.

'Anita, your blood pressure's a bit low so we're going to top up your fluids to stop you going into shock.' Stephanie took off her gloves and wrote up her part of the notes, as well as filling in an X-ray form. 'Once we have the readings of your ECG, we'll get you off to X-Ray to check your shoulder, arm and leg, which may have sustained a break. I can't feel anything solid but, then, that's why we have X-ray machines. We'll get your chest done first, though.'

'Is my shoulder dislocated? I've dislocated that shoulder before.'

'OK.' Stephanie added that bit of information to the X-ray form. 'Even if it is dislocated, we can't relocate it until we've checked the head and neck of the humerus...' she pointed to the top part of the arm and shoulder '...isn't fractured.' She handed the form to Jade. 'Have the orthopaedic surgeon come and see her, but for now she's quite stable. Also, get a parental consent form signed for both her kids so we can treat them as necessary.'

'Already on it,' Jade said, pointing to a form.

The second ambulance was arriving and Stephanie went

to see her next patient, leaving Anita in the capable hands of the nursing staff.

'Nineteen-year-old male, unconscious at the scene, bleeding around the skull, possible fractures to both arms, right leg and several fractured ribs. This guy's car was a mess and we were amazed we actually got him out.'

'Any identification?'

'No. No driver's licence, no medic-alert chain or bracelets. The car he was driving had Queensland number plates.'

'Tourist.' Stephanie had checked his pupils while they'd been speaking and one of the nurses took his vitals. 'Pupils are uneven. What's his BP like?'

'One-sixty over one hundred.'

'Get the neurosurgeon down here. Book him in for magnetic resonance imaging and get the head of the bed elevated to thirty degrees.' As she spoke, another nurse cut away the young man's clothing and draped him with a blanket.

'Gag reflex is absent.'

'Right. Let's intubate.' She grabbed a stethoscope and listened to the patient's chest. 'Breathing sounds quite good, even though there is extensive bruising. He'll need X-rays but I want to find out what's going on around his head first. EEG and ECG to start with.' As she spoke, they worked together to ensure their patient was stable. 'I'll need a complete blood count, coagulation profile, electrolytes, creatinine and arterial blood gases.' Stephanie leaned closer to her patient and breathed in. 'I can't smell alcohol but let's do a general drug and toxicology screen just in case he has another substance in his body we don't know about.'

She felt his arms and identified a break on each ulna. 'They're in almost identical positions.' Next, she felt his legs. 'Right tibia and fibula feel a little displaced, although I'm not too sure.' Steph picked up the paperwork she needed and filled it in. 'How long until neurosurgery gets here?'

'Five more minutes,' someone answered.

'Good.' Without looking up from what she was doing, a smile touched her lips as she felt someone come up behind her. 'Good morning, Stephen.'

'What have you got?' he asked.

'Stephanie?' One of the nurses came in. 'Oliver needs you in TR-2.'

Something in the way the nurse said the words caused Stephanie to feel a little uneasy. She stood, momentarily glancing at her brother.

'What is it?' he asked as he took everything out of her hands.

'I don't know.'

'Go. I'll finish off here.'

When she walked into TR-2, Oliver was standing by the sink, washing his hands. She crossed to his side.

'What can I help you with?'

'Take over the care of this patient. I'm going to check on her brother.'

'Oliver?'

He glanced at her and for that brief moment she saw an almost tortured look in his eyes. 'I won't be long.' He dried his hands and walked out. Stephanie quickly washed her own hands and pulled on a pair of gloves. 'What do we have?'

Sophie crossed to her side and spoke in a muted tone. 'Eight-year-old girl, whiplash, seat-belt bruise and lacerations, breathing a little elevated, but that's to be expected. Query right Colles' fracture. That's about it.'

'Name?'

'Caitlin.'

'OK. Has her father been contacted?'

'Anita's a single mother and they have no family in the district.'

'OK,' Stephanie said again, sighing.

'What's wrong with Oliver?' Sophie asked quietly.

'He's just gone to check on Caitlin's brother.'

'Stephanie, you don't understand. He took one look at the girl, went as white as a sheet and asked for you.'

'Ah.' Stephanie nodded as though things started making sense. 'Oliver has an eight-year-old daughter.'

'Really?' Sophie was surprised. 'Makes sense, then.'

'Let's get to work.' Stephanie walked over to the child. 'Hi, there, Caitlin. I'm Dr Stephanie. Is there anywhere other than your wrist that hurts?'

'I'm really sore everywhere.'

'Understandably. Let's get you something to take away the pain. You've been very brave.'

'Is my mum all right?'

'Yes. I've sent her off to have some X-rays done. She was asking about you and your brother and I told her you were being well looked after.'

'I made them look after Toby first. He's younger than me and he was crying.'

Stephanie checked Caitlin's eyes and felt her head while they spoke. 'You must have been a little scared.'

'I was. I cried in the ambulance but now that I'm here I feel better. That's why I told them to look after Toby first.'

Stephanie smiled. 'That's very kind of you. Now, though, it's your turn to have some attention. Do you know if you're allergic to anything?'

Caitlin's gaze was wide and the brave tone she'd used before faltered a little. 'No. I don't know.'

'That's OK, sweetie. We'll get you sorted out.' Stephanie smiled reassuringly at this young girl who seemed to have taken the world on her shoulders. She gave Caitlin something for the pain and received the obs report from Sophie just as Daisy Brambles walked in.

'Hello, there. Someone call for me?'

'Perfect timing.' Stephanie introduced Caitlin to the pae-diatrician before giving a handover. 'I'll go see how Toby's progressing and also check on your mum, Caitlin. She's going to be happy to hear you're doing just fine.'

Caitlin smiled. 'Thanks, Dr Stephanie, and I love your earrings and hair.'

Everyone chuckled. 'I'm starting to think I should have shaved my head and had it coloured a long time ago. I've never received so many compliments before. I'll come back and let you know how your mum and Toby are.'

Stephanie checked in TR-1 and saw that Stephen was giving a handover to the neurosurgeon on their unnamed patient. Heading to Radiology through the corridors that were full of twists and turns, Stephanie pondered Oliver's reaction to Caitlin. It had to be because Kasey was a similar age.

She caught up with both Toby and Anita in Radiology but couldn't find Oliver. She headed back to A and E and met Caitlin, her barouche being pushed along towards Radiology, and gave her the news of her family.

'But you'll be seeing them both in a minute.'

'Will you check on me later?'

'Of course.' Stephanie smiled reassuringly. 'Dr Daisy's pretty cool, isn't she?'

'She's the best and I love her name. It's what I called my favourite doll.'

'Did you tell her?'

'Yes.' The orderly started pushing the barouche again.

'I'll check on you later,' Stephanie promised as she con-tinued on her way. There was no sign of Oliver in A and E so she went to his office. Again, he wasn't there. A little confused, she backtracked to A and E, knowing she still had a job to do and couldn't spend the rest of her morning searching the hospital for their new boss. He obviously wanted to be alone, so she'd give him the space he needed.

They had a steady stream of patients through A and E until well into the afternoon. Stephen had gone home after the emergency, as he was due back at the hospital for his afternoon-evening shift.

'Still filling in forms?' he asked as he sat beside her at the nurses' station.

'Is it that time already or are you early?'

'Both. I'm about half an hour early so you can knock off.'

'Hmm.' She finished filling in the form.

'What's up, Steph?'

She put her pen down and faced him. 'It's Oliver. I haven't seen him since this morning, although for all I know he could have returned to his office and been working steadily, doing his job all day long. But he certainly hasn't ventured out here.'

'What happened?'

Stephanie briefly told him about Caitlin, who was now settled in the paediatric ward alongside her brother. The nurses had managed to get a private room so Anita could also be put in there, near her children.

'So you haven't seen him since he walked out of TR-2?'

'Nope.'

'Go home. He's a man. He needs space.'

'His daughter is arriving tonight, Stephen. She's on her way here. He should be home to meet her.'

'Well, if he isn't there, someone should be. It would be horrible if your new house guests turned up and no one was there. He's probably been held up in a meeting. You know how it is in that job. Go, Steph.' He held her gaze and immediately Stephanie felt her stress start to lift. 'He's important to you, right?'

Stephanie nodded.

'I'll see if I can find him.'

She threw her arms around her brother's neck. 'You're the best.' She kissed his cheek, then stood. 'I love you, bro.'

Oliver went to lean back in his chair but remembered that wasn't a safe option. He'd worked all day in his office, not wanting to face Stephanie or the feelings that had assailed him on seeing the eight-year-old girl lying there on the barouche. He'd checked up on both children and their mother and was glad to hear the little family was doing so well. The nineteen-year-old man, however, had been transferred to Sydney for further care.

Oliver leaned forward instead of backwards, placing his elbows on the desk and burying his face in his hands. How could he have behaved so unprofessionally? Never before had he been unable to treat a patient—even children.

The knock on his door made him sit up straighter. He hoped it wasn't Stephanie. She'd probably want to psychoanalyse him—all women did. As soon as he had the thought, he dismissed it. He wasn't being fair to Stephanie by tarring her with the same brush as Nadele, but a broken marriage had made him extremely cautious where the fairer sex were concerned.

'Come in,' he called, and was surprised when Stephen entered.

'Got a minute?'

'Only a few. I've just returned from one meeting and unfortunately have another coming up.' He waited while Stephanie's brother came in and sat down opposite him.

'Steph was worried about you.'

It looked as though one twin was as direct as the other. 'Where is she?'

'I made her go home.'

'Good.'

'She tells me your daughter is due there soon.'

'No secrets?'

'She's my sister.'

Stephen made the statement as though it made perfect sense and was the only explanation Oliver deserved. Then again, Oliver had witnessed at first hand the bond brother and sister shared so even if Stephanie didn't tell Stephen everything, he'd eventually pick up on her emotions.

'Does that bother you?' Stephen continued.

'Your closeness?'

'Yes.'

'Yes and no, but I can see it's something I might need to get used to.'

'Meaning?'

'Meaning I like your sister and I'd like to date her.' Oliver held Stephen's gaze.

'Fair enough. What about your daughter?'

'Is this inquisition necessary?'

'I think so, especially if you're interested in my sister.'

'Want to know if my intentions are honourable?'

'Yes, and I'd imagine those intentions included your daughter.'

Oliver nodded. 'I love my daughter, but the past few years haven't been easy for her. I know if I can get Kasey away from her mother's bad influence, I have some hope at establishing a stronger rapport with her.'

'Where does Steph fit into that picture?'

'Right at the moment, I don't know.' Oliver realised this wasn't so much an inquisition but Stephen's attempt at getting to know him better. He appreciated that. It meant the other man was at least willing to give him the benefit of the doubt where Stephanie was concerned.

'And today? With the little girl in the car accident?'

Oliver closed his eyes and shook his head, before looking down at the papers on his desk. 'Seeing that girl there made me realise how important this time with Kasey is. She was travelling today—flying to Australia and then driving from Sydney to here. I looked at that girl and thought, What if this was Kasey? Then every bit of training I've had went out the window and I couldn't remember a thing. It was as though my brain shut down.'

'Vulnerability.' Stephen nodded.

'Exactly.'

'My suggestion—go home and face that vulnerability. Send someone else to the meeting or even ask for it to be cancelled.'

'But I've just started here. It wouldn't look good.'

'It's a small hospital, Oliver. People understand. Go and see for yourself that Kasey is all right.' Stephen stood. 'Steph's good with kids. She'll help you mend your fences. Just go slow with her, that's all I ask.'

'Because she hasn't had much experience?'

Stephen's gaze narrowed. 'Did she tell you that?'

'Yes.'

'I'm impressed, but even more concerned.'

'Why?'

'It means she's becoming more attached to you than I'd anticipated.'

'And that's bad?'

'I don't know yet.' The concern left him. 'Go home, Oliver.'

'Good advice.' Oliver stood and came around the desk to shake Stephen's hand. 'I appreciate you stopping by and your honesty.' He paused then continued. 'Stephanie is…like no other woman I've met. She's come to mean a great deal to me in a short space of time. I'll do my best not to hurt her.'

'I'll hold you to that.'

After Stephen left, Oliver thought over what he'd said and was surprised to realise he meant every word. Stephanie was incredible and he was getting desperate to hold her in his arms and press his lips to hers. Somehow the rest of the world seemed to make sense when he was with Steph and that was something he'd never felt before.

Could it be…love?

Oliver brushed the thought away as ridiculous. He wasn't the type of man to fall in love in such a short space of time and besides, after Nadele and their mockery of a marriage, he'd vowed never to open his heart that deeply again.

He called Darla to put in his apologies for the meeting and was met with no resistance. Then he packed his brief-case, locked his office and drove home.

'Love?' He said the word out loud and shook his head emphatically. No. The feelings he had for Stephanie couldn't possibly be love. Admiration, respect, a growing trust, as well as a growing friendship, but love?

'Impossible.'

CHAPTER EIGHT

STEPHANIE was thankful to get home and quickly rushed around, making sure the place was as tidy as could be.

She was a little puzzled as to why Oliver wasn't there, waiting for Kasey and Mrs Dixon, but there were a few things about Oliver that she didn't understand. He'd declared he wanted permanent custody of Kasey but was this the type of life the child could look forward to? Surely an eight-year-old girl needed more than just an old family housekeeper for support, especially coming to a new country? No doubt Mrs Dixon was as esteemed as Oliver seemed to think she was, but in Stephanie's opinion a child needed parents...and that parent was Oliver.

She thought about Caitlin and how she had seemed more mature than her age. Was that because she was being raised in a one-parent family? Would Kasey be the same? More mature for her age? Stephanie was interested to see.

She boiled the kettle and soon was sitting down, sipping a cup of herbal tea, the soothing sounds of Chopin filling the air. If no one else was going to make Kasey feel welcome, *she* would. She couldn't imagine what loneliness felt like and her imagination was very vivid. Being a twin, she'd never been alone. Even when Stephen had been in a war zone for twelve months, even though she'd felt his desolation and despair, she still hadn't felt alone.

With a burst of energy she decided she was going to make sure Kasey didn't feel alone while she was staying in this house. Stephanie put her cup down and turned the music up. Going to the desk, she turned on the computer and inserted paper into the colour printer.

Soon, she'd finished her transformation. She'd made the beds for both Mrs Dixon and Kasey, printed out some colourful pictures of the latest pop stars she'd downloaded from the internet and stuck these up in Kasey's room, made a WELCOME banner and pinned it up in the lounge room and ordered dinner from one of her favourite restaurants in Katoomba. Although she loved to cook, a girl couldn't do *everything* in so short a time.

As she stepped back to survey her handiwork, she momentarily wondered whether she'd overstepped the mark. After all, Kasey was really nothing to her except Oliver's daughter. Oliver's daughter. Was that the real reason why she'd done all this? Would Kasey see this as a desperate attempt on Stephanie's part to win over her dad?

Stephanie bit her lip, wishing now she'd stopped to think things through a little more. Taking a breath, she let the thought go. No point now, all the work was done…and she was quite proud of it. She heard the crunch of car tyres on the driveway and hoped it was Oliver and not the guests arriving. Crossing to the window, she peered out and breathed an audible sigh of relief as she recognised the silver hire car Oliver had been driving.

He'd no sooner climbed from his car than the sound of another car approaching could be heard. Stephanie watched Oliver turn and head to the edge of the driveway. He put his briefcase down as the hire car came to a halt, and walked over to open the door. A woman, tall and thin with greying hair, climbed from the car. Dignified was the word that came to mind to describe the woman. Although Stephanie was certain Mrs Dixon would take good care of Kasey, would she also let the child have fun?

Stephanie watched with interest as the girl climbed from the car, scooting over to get out the same door as Mrs Dixon. She had red hair which, as she grew older, would darken and become the colour a lot of women envied…women like herself. She smiled but the smile faded as she watched Kasey remain stiff and unmoved as her father came to hug her. Thank goodness Oliver had at least been here when she'd arrived, although it didn't seem to make much difference to Kasey.

The driver brought the bags to the doorstep and Oliver signed a document, no doubt payment for the service, before the driver left. Stephanie swallowed, trying not to fidget or double-check that the banner was straight.

'Don't worry about them, Mrs D. I'll bring them in later. Come in, come in,' she heard Oliver say.

It was then she realised she shouldn't be standing beneath the banner like some idiot welcoming committee. She skidded into the kitchen, grabbed the kettle and headed to the sink. Trying not to pant, she had the tap turned on as they came around the corner. She finished filling the kettle and turned. 'Oh, hi. I'm Stephanie,' she said, pleased at her relaxed and friendly manner. 'Cup of tea?'

'Super,' stated Mrs Dixon.

Kasey stuck out her tongue and made a gagging motion with her finger. Stephanie grinned and switched the kettle on. 'Tea not your thing? Would you like a soft drink? Oh, I mean a *soda*.' She said the word with an American accent but received no reaction from the child.

'Perhaps later,' Oliver said, placing his hand on Kasey's shoulder. The girl shrugged it off and moved away.

Oh, dear. Stephanie grimaced as she met Oliver's gaze. He looked perturbed but was doing his best not to show it. There was a moment of awkward silence until Mrs Dixon saved the day.

'Oh, how splendid,' she said as she noticed the banner in the lounge room. 'Look, Kasey. A WELCOME banner. What a lovely touch, Oliver.'

'Er…yes. Yes.' His eyes widened as he gazed again at Stephanie.

She smiled and winked. 'Why don't you show Kasey and Mrs Dixon their rooms?' she suggested. 'I'll help bring in the bags and then they can freshen up.'

'Yes. Good idea. Right this way, ladies,' he said. A moment later a squeal of excitement came from Kasey.

'I'm allowed to stick posters on the walls?'

'Uh…sure,' came Oliver's uncertain reply, and Stephanie giggled as she retrieved cups and a teapot from the cupboard. Next she headed outside and started hauling in the suitcases. Oliver came to help and took one from her. He put it down and placed both his hands on her shoulders.

'Thank you.' He bent and pressed his lips to hers in a brief and friendly kiss. 'How did you know?'

'Who her favourite pop star was?' She shrugged. 'I didn't. But if she doesn't like the posters, I'll have them in my room. I think he's quite cute.'

Oliver dropped his hands, chuckling as he picked up a bag. 'You're amazing, Stephanie Brooks, and constantly surprising.'

'I presume this is Kasey's bag?'

'Yes.'

'I'll take it in to her. Why don't you deliver Mrs Dixon's luggage and then make her some tea?'

He nodded. 'Do you want a cup?'

'No, thanks. I've just had one.' She headed towards Kasey's room and knocked on the door.

'Come in.' The call was a weary one.

Stephanie opened the door to find the child sitting on the end of the bed, gazing up at the posters. 'Hi. Here's your suitcase.' She hefted it onto the bed. 'Want some help unpacking?'

'No.'

'Ever unpacked before?'

'Of course.' Kasey rolled her eyes. 'I do it every year at boarding school.'

'I forgot that you go to boarding school.'

'That way neither of my parents have to bother dealing with me.'

'That's surprising. I'd say your father's more than willing to…deal with you, as you put it. Otherwise I doubt you'd be here.'

'I'm only here because the courts say I have to be. I spend two weeks every summer holidays with him.'

'What did you do last year?' Stephanie asked.

'We went to Disneyland.'

'For the whole two weeks? How cool.'

Kasey allowed herself a small grin and Stephanie realised the main resemblance between father and daughter were those amazing Bowan blue eyes. 'Yeah, it was kind of cool but it would have been better if one of my friends had been there. I mean, Dad threw up on practically everything that went around in circles.'

Stephanie laughed. 'Really?' She flopped down onto the bed. 'Tell me all about it. I've wanted to go to Disneyland like…for ever.'

'There are so many rides and this summer they've added even more.'

'What about the food? Did you get to eat candy floss?'

'I begged Dad to buy me a stick and he eventually caved in, but I only got one stick for the whole two weeks.'

'Hmm. Something will have to be done about that.'

Kasey giggled, then looked warily at Stephanie. 'Can I touch your hair?'

'Sure.'

'It's spiky.' As she took her hands away, she tinkled Stephanie's earrings. 'These are so wicked.'

'Aren't they? My brother bought them for me. We're twins.'

'You have a *twin* brother? That's way cool. I'd love to have a brother or sister but it isn't going to happen because my parents are divorced. Mom's probably going to get married again soon, but she's said she doesn't want any more kids and said she only had me because Dad wanted a child.'

Stephanie swallowed over the lump in her throat at the child's confession. All she wanted to do was to wrap the child in a huge hug and let her know everything was going to be all right. The bond she was forming with Kasey was as instant as the one she'd formed with the child's father. What was it about these Bowans that just drew her to them?

As though realising she'd said too much, Kasey clammed up and walked around the bed to open her suitcase. Almost desperate to get the previous mood back, Stephanie sat up.

'So, as you're such an expert at unpacking, I thought I might just stay here and get some advice from you while you do it.'

'Advice?' Kasey opened the cupboard and started putting her neatly folded clothes into the drawers.

'Yes. I don't know what to do with my hair. The green colour is starting to grow out. It was much darker when I had it done a few weeks ago. What colour should I do next?'

'Really? You're going to colour your hair again?'

'Well, I'm not. The hairdresser is.'

'That's so not fair. You grown-ups get it so easy. You want to do something, so you do it. I want to change the colour of my hair but I'm not allowed to.'

'Your colour is fantastic.'

'It's horrible. Girls at school call me Carrot Top and Orangeade.'

'Isn't that a drink?'

'Hello! Of course it's a drink.'

'But in a few more years your hair is going to darken

and be the most beautiful colour. My hair used to be almost the same colour as yours before I had it all shaved off.'

'Why did you? I thought maybe you'd been sick and that's why your hair was short.'

'No.' She explained about the 'Shave for a Cure' campaign.

'Wow. That's so cool.'

'My point is that I paid to have my hair coloured the same colour as yours. Many women do. It's the *in* colour.'

'Really?' She shrugged. 'I don't care. I hate it.'

'Are you going to give me advice or just whinge?'

'Whinge?' Kasey was puzzled at the word.

'Whine.'

'I wasn't whining.'

'Sounded like it to me, Kasey.' Stephanie smiled, taking away the severity of her words.

The girl grimaced.

'What?'

'I don't like my name.'

'Oh? What *do* you like?'

'Kaz. It's what my friends at school call me.'

'Okey-dokey. I'll call you Kaz and you call me Steph.'

The smile was back. 'Deal.' There was a knock at the door and after Kasey gave her consent, Oliver opened the door.

'What are you two doing in here?'

'Deciding important girl stuff,' Stephanie said, and crossed to the door.

'Such as?'

Stephanie stood back and looked him up and down. 'I don't see you wearing a dress, Dr Bowan, which means you're not a girl.'

'Hey. You're not wearing a dress either and your hair is shorter than mine.'

Stephanie giggled. 'Oh, just go. We'll be out in a minute.'

Go and drink your tea.' She gave him a little shove backwards and winked at him again. The smile he gave her in response had her insides melting, and as he relented and left, she shut the door, leaning against it in a dreamy fashion.

She sighed then crossed to the bed again. 'Now, where were we? Oh, yes, you were going to pick a new colour for my hair.'

'Are you dating my dad?'

'Well, that's certainly straight to the point. No. I'm not dating your dad.' She smiled. 'But I'd like to.'

'That's gross. He's so old.'

Stephanie laughed. 'So am I.'

'Yeah, but you don't act it.'

'So I've been told.' She grinned, then added, 'Your dad and I work together at the hospital.' She briefly told Kasey about the fire and the mix-up in accommodation.

'That's so sad.'

'But now I get to pick out all new stuff for my new house *and* I had to go and buy all new clothes.'

'Wow. Need help shopping?'

'You like shopping?'

Kasey stood up and twirled around. 'I *am* wearing a dress, aren't I?'

Both of them giggled. 'Come on,' Stephanie said once Kasey had finished unpacking. 'Let me put your suitcase away for you and we'll go see what your dad wants.'

At the door, Kasey said quite seriously, 'Leave it green for a bit longer. I've never met anyone with green hair before. The snobby girls at school are so going to freak when I tell them.'

'OK. Green it stays for a while longer. Thanks.'

The following week was quite interesting and Stephanie found she thoroughly enjoyed spending time with Kasey.

'You know she prefers to be called Kaz, don't you?' sh
asked Oliver one evening as they sat in the hospital cafe
teria, enjoying a coffee-break. The hospital was alive wit
rumours of the personal relationship between Stephanie an
Oliver but the truth was he'd made no effort to kiss her fo
over a week. Instead, they'd both worked hard at maintain
ing their agreement to be just friends and Stephanie ha
found she liked being Oliver's friend…very much.

'I know *you* call her that but I thought it was just
nickname you'd come up with.'

'No. She told me she prefers it.'

'Oh.'

'Try it.'

Oliver shook his head. 'I can't. She hasn't told me.'

'So? I've just told you.'

'I don't want to upset her.'

'You won't. Trust me. She's already started thawing an
I noticed this morning at breakfast she actually laughed a
one of your teasing jokes.'

Oliver's smiled brightened at the memory. 'Yes, she did
didn't she?' He took a deep breath and slowly exhaled. 'A
lot of Kasey's positive attitude is thanks to you.'

'As you said, she was responding better to stranger
when she arrived.' Stephanie shrugged and drained he
coffee-cup. 'I just filled that gap.'

'I think she'd hardly call you a stranger now. I heard
you both giggling in her room last night.'

Stephanie smiled and reached across the table to take hi
hand. 'She is so much like you, Oliver. She's so easy to
get along with.'

He laced his fingers with hers. 'Whatever you do, don'
tell her that.'

'Why not? She needs to feel she's at least inherited
something from her parents—it gives her a sense of worth.
When she becomes a teenager, she'll deny all connections

to you but now…right now she's desperate to attach herself to either you or Nadele.'

At the mention of his ex-wife, both of them sobered. 'Have you heard anything from Nadele in the last few days?'

'Yes. Another email came through saying she was definitely going to take it further.' Oliver shook his head with determination. 'These past few days, seeing Kasey beginning to thaw, have just increased my resolve to fight harder.'

'What about a permanent housekeeper? If you were to get custody of her, wouldn't that be a stipulation of the court? Mrs Dixon has only agreed to be in Australia with Kasey for the duration of her stay.'

'That's something I'm still working on.' He let go of her hand and stood. 'This *has* to work out. I'm not letting her go back to that boarding school. I can tell she hates it.'

'Why don't you try talking to Kaz about all this?'

'She's only—'

'Don't. Stop treating her like a child—'

'She *is* a child, Stephanie.'

'Without a brain, I was going to say. Kasey is a highly intelligent girl, Oliver. She takes after her father.' Stephanie smiled as she stood and carried their coffee-cups over to where the dirty dishes were stacked. 'Ask her what *she* wants. At least, that way, if she wants to stay here with you, you have something to work with. She has every right to go before the court and give her own opinion.'

'But what if she *doesn't* want to stay?'

Stephanie's smile increased and she waggled her eyebrows up and down. 'Then we need to do some fancy footwork. Come on, we need to get back to work.'

As they walked along the corridor, Oliver glanced across at her. 'What do you have in mind?'

'For a start, this Friday let's take her out and give her a

special day. Mrs Dixon as well. Just as a way of saying thank you to both of them.'

He stopped walking and she followed suit. 'Does this have anything to do with you getting Mrs Dixon out the house so you can win your bet?'

'See how well you know me?' It was true. In the week they'd just shared, the bond between them had increased and on several occasions they'd been able to read each other's minds.

'I don't know whether to sabotage or support it. If I agree, I have the opportunity of becoming closer to my daughter, but I'll be stuck doing the rosters.'

'Let me give you some advice—you're going to be doing the rosters whether you win the bet or not.'

He laughed and continued walking before he gave in to the urge to haul her into his arms, spin her around in the corridor and plant a lip-smacking kiss where it definitely belonged. 'What do you have in mind?'

'Well, if the weather's fine, I thought we might head to Lithgow and take her on the Zig Zag Railway, then we can head to Jenolan Caves and do a cave walk or two, perhaps have a bite to eat in Caves House and then head back towards Blackheath and have afternoon tea at the Megalong Tearooms. The tearooms have the most yummy meals and snacks and you can sit outside in a lovely garden where you feel all the stress of the real world simply disappear.'

'Sounds like a very grand day out.'

'Yes. Seeing some of the wonderful sights this area has to offer.'

'And you're planning to get Mrs D. to come along for it all?'

'She won't be able to resist.'

'How do you know?' They walked into A and E towards the nurses' station.

'Because it'll be educational, and if there's one thing I've

oticed about Mrs Dixon, it's her determination to make
his holiday in Australia as educational as possible for both
erself and Kasey.'

As Friday morning dawned, Oliver marvelled at the won-
er of Stephanie. True to her plan, which she'd outlined to
Mrs Dixon in great *educational* detail, the weather seemed
erfect. A little cool but the sky was blue and the sun was
hining.

Kasey was as excited as he'd ever seen her, and not for
he first time he realised how much he owed to Stephanie.
Before he'd come to Katoomba, his life had felt so con-
icted, so…in a mess, and now, less than two weeks later,
is daughter was laughing and smiling at him, Mrs Dixon
eemed more at ease than he'd ever seen her before and all
ecause of the infectious spirit of one woman.

Stephanie was dancing in the kitchen to a tune on the
adio and Kasey was watching. Then, to his surprise, Kasey
oined in the chorus, singing with an amazing voice and
oving up and down the small kitchen beside Steph. Oliver
vas stunned.

'Kaz. You have an amazing voice.' The admiration was
lear in his tone and Kasey beamed.

'Thanks. I started taking singing lessons last term.'

'Why didn't I know about this?'

She shrugged but the old look of shutting him out came
cross her face. Oliver stood and walked over to her, plac-
ng his hands on her shoulders. 'Please, Kaz,' he said softly.
Tell me why you didn't want me to know.'

Kasey shrugged. 'Mom always says you hate frivolous
hings.'

'What?' He was shocked and glanced past Kasey at
Stephanie. She gave him an encouraging look and turned
own the radio, eager to see how Oliver dealt with this
nformation. 'How is singing frivolous?'

Kasey shrugged.

'But last year we went to Disneyland. Surely that shoul show you I like frivolous things.'

'Mom said she begged you to take me and that you fi nally gave in only to stop her from hounding you.'

'What?' Oliver found it hard to swallow his temper an slammed a fist onto the bench, making both Kasey an Stephanie jump. 'Sorry.' He raked a hand through his hai and shook his head. He realised he couldn't tell her th situation had been completely reversed. He'd *wanted* t take Kasey to Disneyland but Nadele hadn't agreed, sayin it was a waste of money and he'd be better off buyin Kasey an expensive present to show her how much h cared. Yet, if he told Kasey that now, he'd be doing exactl what Nadele had done. If he put Nadele down, he'd b sinking to her level, and he wasn't going to give his ex wife the satisfaction.

'I had a fantastic time at Disneyland, and do you kno why?'

'Because I didn't force you to go on all those rides. Kasey's words were a statement and one which she whole heartedly believed. She lowered her head and looked at th ground.

'No! I had a fantastic time...' he lifted her chin so thei gazes could meet '...because I was with *you.*'

'Really?' Hope flared in the little girl's eyes. It was a though she desperately wanted to believe him but wasn' sure she could trust him.

'*Yes.*' He gently pushed some hair out of her face 'Kasey, I love you. Don't you know that?'

'Well...Steph told me you did but I wasn't sure.'

Oliver's gaze flicked up to meet Stephanie's, then h laughed. 'Are you crying, Dr Brooks?'

Stephanie sniffed and reached for a tissue. 'Don't min me,' she said as she blew her nose, making Kasey laugh

'You two just keep going. I'll make some popcorn because this is an excellent show.'

'Popcorn for breakfast?' Oliver queried, picking up his daughter for the first time in many years and holding her close. To his absolute delight, Kasey put her arms around his neck.

'Hey—don't knock it till you've tried it, mate. Besides, popcorn for breakfast is…well…frivolous.' She grinned at him and was surprised when he came over and placed his free arm about her shoulders.

'Steph, you are one in a million.'

'Actually,' she said as she gazed up at him, 'that's one in a billion, if you don't mind.'

Oliver couldn't help himself. Still holding Kasey, he lowered his head and pressed his lips to Stephanie's.

'Oh, ick!' Kasey groaned and wriggled free from his grasp. 'I thought you two weren't dating?'

'We aren't,' Stephanie said.

'I don't see why not,' Mrs Dixon said as she walked into the kitchen. 'Both of you want to.'

'She's right,' Kasey added, as she walked around the bench and climbed onto one of the stools. 'Now, are we going out today or are you two going to make *moochy* faces at each other?'

'Moochy faces?' Oliver reluctantly let Stephanie go and came to sit by his daughter.

'You figure it out, Dad.'

'Hmm, I think I already have.' He looked across at Stephanie again and to his surprise she winked at him. It brought the smile back to his face. 'Right. Let's have breakfast and get this day rolling. Frivolity—here we come.'

Stephanie quickly excused herself and rushed to her room, closing the door firmly and leaning against it. Then, as though her legs were made of jelly, she walked across to the mirror and looked at her reflection.

Her blue eyes were wide with incredulity and she shook her head slowly as she acknowledged the truth of her emotions. 'It shouldn't have happened,' she told her reflection softly. 'How could it have happened?'

Quite easily, came the answer from her heart, and she realised it was the truth. From the moment she'd met Oliver, she'd known there was something different about him. There was amazing chemistry between them, they'd become good friends and she'd helped him mend some fences with his daughter. It was no wonder she'd fallen in love with the guy, but the main problem was, what on earth was she supposed to do about it?

CHAPTER NINE

'STEPH?' Oliver called as he knocked on her bedroom door five minutes later. 'Stephen's on the phone.'

'Oh.' Stephanie crossed to her bedside table and checked her cellphone. Closing her eyes, she shook her head, realising she'd forgotten to charge it again. 'Uh…' She cleared her throat. 'I'll be right there.'

Straightening her shoulders, she gave herself a quick check in the mirror, then laughed at her own antics. Oliver wouldn't be able to see what she'd discovered. It wasn't as though she had the words, 'I'M IN LOVE WITH YOU' tattooed to her forehead. Stephen would know, hence his phone call, but Oliver—he'd be clueless. She opened the door. At least, she *hoped* he'd be clueless.

Taking a deep breath, she walked out and picked up the phone. 'Hi. I forgot to charge my cellphone.'

'What's going on?'

'Uh…nothing much. We're leaving soon for a day out, seeing the sights.' She knew her voice sounded over-bright and knew Stephen would pick up on that.

'You can't talk, eh? OK. Well, have a nice day and I'll talk to you later. Love you, sis.'

'Love you, too,' she said, and hung up. She glanced across at Oliver and was surprised to find him looking at her. He knows! No, he can't know. I didn't even know until ten minutes ago. How could he possibly know?

'So…' She clicked her fingers, knowing she was behaving uncharacteristically. 'What's for breakfast? Can I help, Mrs D.?'

'Thank you, Stephanie. That would be appreciated.'

Glad to have something to do, Stephanie eventually found her usual fun-loving attitude and soon had everyone laughing. They all had a good day and after eating lunch at Caves House at Jenolan, they took the scenic route back to Blackheath. At the Megalong Tearooms down in the winding but picturesque Megalong Valley, Mrs Dixon sighed.

'I have to confess, dear, that I'm not an outdoors person but this area is just divine. It's extremely pretty and reminds me of home.'

'Whereabouts are you from?' Stephanie asked, giving Oliver a wink. She'd definitely won the bet and the rosters were no longer hers to worry about.

'Cumbria, dear. Have you ever been there?'

'Not to Cumbria. I only made it as far as London.' Stephanie toyed with her cup, looking out to where Kasey was playing on the grass with the owners' dog.

'All the tourist spots and nightclubs?' Oliver asked. Stephanie met his gaze for a second before shaking her head, unable to believe that tears were welling in her eyes. 'Steph?' He took her hand in his.

'I went to London to say goodbye to my mother. She died three days after I arrived.'

Oliver squeezed her hand, pain reflected in his eyes.

'Oh, my dear. I'm sorry to hear that,' Mrs Dixon offered. 'And your father?'

'He died when Stephen and I were teenagers.'

'So it's just you and your brother, then?'

'Yes.'

'Then it's nice that you're both so close,' she finished with a smile. 'I've given up all hope of Oliver and Augustus becoming friends.'

'I'm glad to hear that, Mrs D.,' Oliver said, still holding Stephanie's hand. It appeared he was in no hurry to let it

o. 'Because that means it's safe to tell you that Augustus
s pursuing Nadele.'

Mrs Dixon was momentarily stunned before she nodded.
'Well, at least they're a better fit than you and Nadele. Why
ou ever married that woman in the first place is beyond
1e.'

'Call it an experiment that went wrong.'

'Is that what it was?' Stephanie asked.

'No.'

'More like your brain that went wrong,' Mrs Dixon
dded, and Stephanie laughed.

'Either way, it was a long time ago and is in the past.'

'Yes, you're right, dear. I apologise for mentioning it. At
:ast,' Mrs Dixon said, as she stood, 'you're making better
hoices now.' She patted Stephanie's free hand before
valking off.

'Well, well,' Oliver said, as he shifted around to come
nd sit on the bench seat next to Stephanie. 'It appears
ou've been given the seal of approval by Mrs D.'

'Hmm. I take it that's a good thing?'

Oliver smiled and leaned in to kiss her on the nose.
That's a very good thing.' He pulled back, the smile
lowly slipping from his face as he held her gaze. 'Have I
1entioned that I find you mind-numbingly attractive?'

Stephanie felt the butterflies begin to whirl in her stom-
ch. It happened every time Oliver looked at her that way,
nd today was no exception. In fact, today everything had
ntensified but she'd hardly expected less, considering she'd
cknowledged she was in love with the man. She sighed
nd decided to enjoy the sensation rather than fight it. So
vhat? She loved Oliver and he was looking at her now as
1ough he wanted to kiss her senseless. Who was she to
eny him?

His gaze flicked from her eyes to her mouth, lingering
n the mouth in a sweet, visual caress. It was just as if he'd

touched her, and when his gaze returned to hers, she knew he could read the desire there…that she *wanted* his touch, his lips to be on hers.

'Maybe we should try dating,' he murmured as he gradually closed the gap. 'It's there, Steph. The attraction is there and it keeps getting stronger.' His breath fanned her face and her lips parted in hungry anticipation, needing and wanting him with every agonising second they were apart. 'Friends is fun, but…'

'But this is better.'

'Mmm.' His fingers caressed her cheek and her eyelids fluttered closed as a wave of tingles spread over her. He was intoxicating and even though they'd tried to slow things down, the increasing pressure was too much for either of them to deny.

Opening her eyes, she looked at his mouth. So full and rich and just waiting for her. It felt so right. Everything about them… It was as though they were destined and she knew intuitively they were meant to be.

'Oliver.' His name had barely left her lips when his mouth was finally pressed to hers. Both of them gasped then relaxed into the kiss, unable to believe how incredible the chemistry between them was.

His hands came up to cup her face, her earrings tinkling. His body language spoke of need, of greed and of possession, and he didn't care. He couldn't believe the way this woman seemed to make him forget all rationality. He'd never felt so…consumed before, and the more he got to know her, the more he desired her.

Her mouth was sublime, the perfect fit to his, opening beneath his, matching his hunger and passion to the fullest extent. How could he not want more? They were two halves that made a whole and although he'd expected the revelation to shock him, it only made him deepen the kiss, wanting to prove to her that she was special.

Until now, the kisses they'd shared had been merely a prelude to what they were both experiencing. How could he have not realised sooner the intensity of her feelings for this man? Even in the last few seconds, since his mouth had been pressed to hers, her emotions had grown. They were meant to be and that was all she could focus on. The rest of the world was out of focus—there was only the two of them, and that was fine by her.

Stephanie pulled back, gasping for breath, leaning on him for support. 'Oliver.'

He swallowed. 'I know.' He held her, his hands gently caressing her back. 'You know, I think that's the first time I've kissed you that we haven't been interrupted.'

Stephanie merely sighed, breathing in the fresh, spicy scent of him.

'Let's take a chance, Steph. Let's date.'

She was silent for a moment and he wondered whether he'd heard him. Eventually, she spoke.

'I don't know if I can.'

'Date me?' Oliver pulled back to look at her, a little perplexed. 'Can't you feel the buzz between us?'

'Is it a bee?' she asked, and he gave her a small grin for her attempt at humour.

'Steph. We're good together.' Although she'd said she was inexperienced as far as relationships went, didn't she realise how incredible it was between them? Didn't she realise that relationships like this didn't just fall off trees? Come on. Let's try dating.'

'I don't know if I can,' she repeated, and edged away from him a little. Stephanie could almost hear the blood pumping faster around her body as she met his gaze.

'Why not?'

'Because I'm in love with you,' she blurted. She watched as the rapture they'd just shared was washed away. 'Yes, I want to date you but I want more than just dates, Oliver.'

'What do you want?' He frowned a little, uncertain how to take the bomb she'd just dropped on him.

'The fairy-tale. Isn't that what every girl wants when she falls in love?'

'Are you sure it's real love?'

Stephanie felt her hackles rise and the look in Oliver' eyes told her he realised he'd said the wrong thing. 'I may be a novice when it comes to relationships, Oliver, but I'm not a novice when it comes to reading my own emotions. At least I'm honest enough to admit it.'

'What's that supposed to mean? That I'm not?'

She stood and took a few steps away from him.

'Stephanie, I don't know you that well.' The look she gave him would have withered even the toughest weed, and once more he realised he'd said the wrong thing. He shook his head and raked a hand through his hair. 'Can't we just try dating? Getting to know each other even better?'

When she didn't reply, he clambered from the bench seat and came to stand before her. 'Look, Steph. I've been there. Marriage. It wasn't good.'

'I've heard it isn't good if you're married to the wrong person, and how dare you compare me to Nadele? I may not know the woman but, from what I've heard you, Kasey and Mrs Dixon say, I'm nothing like her. Anyway, this has nothing to do with her. This is between the two of us, Oliver. I understand your need to want to slow things down, to date, to get to know each other more, but I also thought you should know the truth. I'm not into keeping secrets.'

Stephanie took a deep breath then shrugged. 'You're right. There is something amazing between us, but the question you need to ask yourself is just how far you're willing to take things. I'm not going to date you if it's just an interlude for you. I'm also not going to apologise for my feelings. You're so incredible.' She smiled shyly at him. 'How could I resist falling in love with you?'

*   *   *

It seemed, on the drive home, that Stephanie was more than happy to keep up a friendly banter with Mrs Dixon and Kasey, but the instant they arrived home she headed to her room and that was the last he saw of her for the day.

Oliver needed space. Everything had happened so fast and his feelings for Stephanie were so confusing. On one hand, he resented her blurting out the fact that she was in love with him. It made him want to retreat into his cave where no one could get at him, but somehow she still managed to affect him—even there. On the other hand, he was aware of the precious gift she'd given him. She loved him! It thrilled him and totally freaked him at the same time.

Could he go there again? Open himself up to the hurt, pain and humiliation that could come with marriage? Unfortunately for Stephanie, he'd seen the worst side possible where marriage was concerned. She was right, though. She wasn't Nadele and he had to realise that any relationship he might have with Stephanie would be completely different. *He* was a completely different man to the one who'd married Nadele all those years ago, so surely that was proof enough that he and Stephanie wouldn't fail.

Why was it that just as one part of his life finally settled down, another part exploded, leaving him to gather the pieces and try and figure out which way to put them back together again? Kasey, or Kaz as he'd started to call her, had opened up to him. She was becoming more generous with her hugs and he marvelled at the difference in her in such a short space of time. Was it because he'd told her he loved her? That she could *see* that he loved her? Was it because Stephanie had instantly tapped into the child's psyche and guided him through the minefield of emotions until Kasey had been willing to let him in?

Perhaps the vast distance between child and mother was a contributing factor. Usually Nadele had Kasey either side of his court-appointed time, but this year Kasey knew it would be quite a while before she'd have to see her mother again…and if he had his way, it would be a great deal longer.

He picked up the latest information from his solicitor and knew this was something he could deal with. It would mean a trip to Sydney to work out the final details, but if everything went to plan, he might have permanent custody of Kasey within the next few weeks. It was better than he'd hoped and it was all thanks to Augustus.

During the next week, Oliver watched with delight as Kasey continued to blossom. She made him happy and proud and as it looked as though her stay in Australia would be permanent, he decided the time was right to move on. He contacted the estate agent and started looking at a few properties. Kasey, of course, came with him as she had a right to say where they would live. She usually had a lot of questions about things, but today—nearly a week after their wonderful day travelling around the Blue Mountains—her questions were more about Stephanie than the accommodation.

'Why do we have to move?'

'We've been over this, Kaz. The place we're staying in doesn't belong to us.'

'What about Steph?'

'Stephanie's house will be rebuilt soon.'

'Will she be moving back there?'

'Of course. It will be her house.' Oliver inspected the kitchen cupboards while they spoke, but his mind was definitely not on what he was doing. Kasey's questions had triggered in him a response to delay everything—delay moving out of the house they were in now and also asking Stephanie to hold the future construction of her home. He had no right to do either, but that didn't stop him feeling a need to hold on to things just the way they were.

Although, if he was completely honest, he'd acknowl-
edge the relationship between him and Stephanie was becoming more strained as the days passed. It wasn't that they
were being uncivil to each other but that they were killing
each other with polite kindness. He also noticed she stayed
out of his way as much as possible.

'Are you going to see if Mom will let me stay in
Australia for ever?'

As far as Oliver was concerned, the question came from
left field, and as he turned around he knocked his head on
the corner of the cupboard door. He frowned, rubbing the
spot. Although he'd been working to bring about such a
resolution, he hadn't discussed it with Kasey. Stephanie had
told him he should but, quite frankly, he'd been procrasti-
nating…not wanting to break the bond he'd formed with
Kasey.

He looked at her. 'Would you like that?'

'Would I get to live with you all the time?'

'Full time. One house, same bed every night.'

Kasey's eyes widened. 'I wouldn't have to go to boarding school any more?'

'Not if you didn't want to. There are some good boarding
schools in Sydney and you could come home every weekend, but only if that's what you wanted.'

Kasey looked away. 'I guess I could go.'

'No. No,' Oliver implored and made her look at him.
'Kaz, I *want* you with me—all the time. I don't want you
to go to boarding school, but some kids like being away
from their parents. Your mother always told me you loved
boarding school.'

'What?'

Dawning realisation hit Oliver between the eyes. 'Oh,
Kaz.' He dragged her to him. 'I've been such a fool. I
should have fought harder for you.' He went down on one

knee and looked at her. 'Do you want to come and live here with me?'

'And Steph? Yes. I want that more than anything.'

'Well...' Oliver swallowed. 'You'll be able to see Steph. I know she wants to go shopping with you.'

'Yeah. She told me.' Kasey walked over to the kitchen bench and leaned on it. 'Aren't you going to marry Steph?'

'Kaz, it's not that simple.'

'Why isn't it? Don't you love her?'

Oliver slowly stood. He'd asked himself the same question over and over since Stephanie had said those words to him last week. Did he love her? He wasn't sure...wasn't sure he could trust his judgement where loving her was concerned. All the emotions he'd felt when his marriage to Nadele had fallen apart had reared their ugly heads again. He'd thought he was over it all, that he'd worked through the rejection years ago, but now, when it became evident he had to make a choice, he felt paralysed.

'I don't know,' he finally answered his daughter. 'Things are a *little* complicated.'

That, he thought, was the understatement of the year.

On Thursday, Stephanie decided she'd had enough and after the weekend she'd take Stephen up on his offer of hospitality. Even though she knew Stephen needed the space right now, she couldn't help it. Being so close yet so far from Oliver was making her ill. She wasn't sleeping or eating properly, and she just needed to get away.

Thankfully, she had the weekend off and thought a trip to Sydney would be just what she needed. She could catch up with a few friends from med school, have some retail therapy and perhaps get a new colour on her hair. She wasn't sure whether to go with something wild and dramatic—like purple or fuchsia-pink—or whether to just go red-orange like Kasey's. She must remember to discuss it with Kasey before she went.

After work, she met Nicolette for coffee, pleased to hear her friend was no longer fighting her attraction towards Stephen.

'Yes. I love him. Satisfied?'

Stephanie grinned. 'You'd better believe it. You're so perfect for him.'

'If only he would see that.'

Stephanie sighed, knowing exactly how her friend felt. She managed to neatly sidestep any questions regarding Oliver and her current situation, knowing that although Nicolette would be supportive and encouraging, the fact was, she just wasn't ready to discuss it.

When she arrived home, it was to find Oliver holding his daughter in his arms and dancing around the room to Chopin. She presumed by the wonderful aroma wafting through the house that Mrs Dixon was in the kitchen. She stood by the doorframe, watching them both, Kasey giggling as she held on tight. It was a picture-perfect moment and the magnitude of her emotions swamped her. She swallowed over the lump in her throat, telling herself now was not the time as she fought back the tears.

Seeing Oliver and Kasey getting along so well made Stephanie realise she was no longer needed. Initially Oliver had needed her help—now he didn't. His relationship with Kasey had gone from strength to strength in a very short space of time but she was glad she'd been able to bring them together.

Tonight she would tell him she'd be moving out. She had no problem with him staying in the house for as long as he needed to, even though she knew he'd been looking at other houses during the week. Oliver hadn't said a word but Kasey had. Stephanie had tried to be positive as the eight-year-old had told her about some of the houses she'd looked at with her father, but the realisation that her job in Oliver's life was done was becoming painfully obvious.

The staff at work had accepted the changes Oliver had made, a little reluctantly at first but now everyone could see how everything was working better and faster. Again, the staff had looked to her for guidance and she'd given it, supporting Oliver all the way.

Even at work, she was obsolete.

Realising she was fighting a losing battle with the tears that kept threatening, she hurried up the corridor to her bedroom, hoping she hadn't been seen. She blew her nose and took some deep breaths, and a moment later a knock sounded on her door.

'Steph?' It was Kasey. 'Can I come in?'

Stephanie cleared her throat and pasted on a smile. 'Sure.'

The girl bounced into the room, excitement radiating through ever pore. 'Guess what? Dad's going to take me to Sydney for the weekend.'

Stephanie was unable to control her reaction to the news. In fact, her face must have looked very bleak because Kasey said, 'What's wrong? Aren't you excited? I am!'

Stephanie turned away, cross with herself for not being able to control her emotions. 'That sounds great. You'll have a wonderful time.' How could Oliver do this to her? *She* was the one who'd planned to go to Sydney for a break, and right now she desperately needed it. If he was going to Sydney then she'd have to stay here and wait for her next weekend off.

'Oh, but you're coming, too.'

'What?' Stephanie spun around to face her.

'We're going shopping, remember?'

'Uh…but you're going with your father.'

'Yes, but he doesn't know the first thing about clothes.'

Kasey twirled around, the skirt of her dress flaring out. 'We're girls. We know how to find a bargain.'

Stephanie laughed, unable to help herself. She sat on the edge of the bed and motioned for Kasey to come over. The little girl came and put her arms around Stephanie's neck. 'It does sound wonderful, but I can't come.'

'Why not?' a deep, masculine voice asked from the doorway. 'Kaz has her heart set on it and I've made sure you're not rostered on this weekend.' He took two steps into her room. 'And don't ask me to change the rosters, Stephanie Brooks, because you know how horrible and frustrating that can be.'

She smiled in spite of her turbulent emotions. 'Yes.'

'You'll come?'

Stephanie pondered it for a moment. She'd still be able to catch up with her friends and she'd never been shopping with an eight-year-old before, so it might just be exciting. She and Kasey could shop and Oliver could do his business. She might not even need to see that much of him. 'Is Mrs Dixon coming?'

'Er…' He seemed surprised at the question. 'I think so. I'm sure she would.'

She glanced down at Kasey who was grinning expectantly. 'OK. I'll come.'

'Yay!' Kasey danced around the room and Stephanie marvelled at the change in the child who had first walked into this house. Mrs Dixon called them to dinner and they all headed out of her room—Oliver waiting, as a gentleman should, for the women to precede him.

'Thank you,' he said, his breath tingling down her spine. She hadn't realised he was so close. 'You've made her night.'

Stephanie shivered but didn't turn to look at him…it would have been too dangerous. She breathed in, loving his unique scent, amazed at what he could do to her just by being so close. He wasn't even touching her and she was a quivering mass of jelly. How on earth was she going to survive the heartbreak she could feel coming? It had been nearly a week since she'd told Oliver she loved him, and yet here they were, still doing the same dance, a dance which she knew wouldn't end in commitment.

He wanted to date her but beyond that they hadn't discussed a thing. Part of her wanted to say that she'd date him and not expect anything else, but she just couldn't. She was an old-fashioned girl waiting for a man with old-fashioned values. It was that simple.

When Friday dawned, her alarm clock buzzing in her ear, she groaned, switched it off, turned over and buried her head beneath the pillow. She wasn't due at work until just after lunch so why was her alarm clock bugging her now?

A moment later, there was knocking at her bedroom door. 'Huh?' She lifted her head. 'Go away. I'm sleeping.'

She heard Oliver chuckle. 'Can I come in?'

'No, you can't,' she said.

'Steph, it's almost midday, and you're due at work in an hour.'

'What?' She sat bolt upright and glared at her clock and it confirmed what Oliver was saying. 'Why didn't you wake me up sooner?'

'I thought that's why you had an alarm clock. Listen, I've just dropped home to have lunch with Kaz—and do I have to have this conversation through the door?'

Huffily, Stephanie gathered the doona around her. 'Fine. Come in, then.'

So he did, and stopped just inside the doorway, staring at her in the big bed. It was messy, with a few pillows on the floor and the doona untucked. Testament to a sleepless night. *Snap!* Stephanie, though, looked the most incredible, the most stunning he'd ever seen her, and he swallowed uickly, watching how she took in everything about him. Belatedly, he realised she was speaking. 'Pardon?'

'What do you want, Oliver?'

'You sound tired.'

'I am.' Thank goodness he hadn't said she *looked* tired, otherwise she would have thrown him out of her room and possibly out of her friend's house. 'Your point for barging in here was…?'

'Yes.' He cleared his throat and forced himself to look away, unable to believe how she could turn his mind to mush just by being in the same room as him. 'I received a phone call from my solicitor this morning. Augustus has persuaded Nadele to relinquish custody of Kaz.'

Stephanie's jaw dropped in surprise before a smile lit her features. 'That's…' She shook her head, her mind not up to deciding which adjective was appropriate to describe her feelings. 'You must be thrilled.'

'I came home to give Kaz the good news.'

'She's happy about it?'

'Yes. There are still a lot of formalities to wrap up.'

'Hence the trip to Sydney?'

'Yes. Kaz needs to have a conversation with my solicitor just to confirm this is what *she* wants. Once the papers are through, we sign them and seal them and deliver them. I don't know to whom, but deliver them we shall.'

His good mood was infectious and Stephanie found her earlier fatigue lifting after just a few minutes in his presence. They would be so perfect together. Why couldn't he see that?

'Was there anything else?'

'Huh? Er…no. Just wanted to tell you the good news.'

Stephanie nodded. 'I appreciate it. Now I think I'd better get up and get ready for work.'

'Of course.' He headed to the door then stopped and

turned back to face her. 'Do you think we can leave by ten o'clock tomorrow?'

Stephanie had already started moving and when he turned back to face her she had just put her feet on the floor, her short nightie revealing a generous amount of leg. Oliver found himself staring, his mouth suddenly going dry.

'That's fine.'

He heard her reply but it didn't compute. 'Oliver, unless you plan to marry me, I suggest you stop looking at me like that and get out of here as fast as you can.'

'Marry?' He raised his gaze to hers. He saw a mixture of repressed anger and desire and realised she was at the boiling point, ready to explode. 'Right. Sorry.'

'It worked,' she muttered gloomily, after he'd closed the door and left her in peace. 'Peace? Ha!' She forced herself to go through the routine of showering and dressing and, after she'd eaten something, congratulating Kasey on the verdict, Stephanie's anxiety increased. Surely the situation between herself and Oliver wasn't affecting her this badly?

'Are you all right?' Oliver asked.

'I'm not sure.'

He raised his eyebrows and went to put his hand on her forehead, but she shied away.

'It's not that. I think I'll give Stephen a call. I won't be long and I certainly won't be late for my shift.'

'I have no doubt about that,' Oliver said. He said goodbye to Kasey and Mrs Dixon and headed out the door. Stephanie reached for her cellphone and went back to her room for a bit of privacy. Stephen answered on the first ring.

'Hi, Steph.'

'Hi, yourself. Having fun?'

'Not really.'

'I thought as much. This is just a quick call because I'm

about to walk out the door and head to work. So what's going on? More angst over Nic?'

'I doubt it will ever go away,' he mumbled.

'It'll only go away if you face it. Have you told her how you feel?'

'The attraction is mutual, Steph.'

'It's amazing that you can be more stubborn than me. I'm not talking about the attraction. Do you love her?' Stephanie waited, amazed at how similar their situations were. Oliver seemed to be as stubborn as her brother.

'I don't know,' Stephen finally answered.

'Well…' she drawled. 'That's an improvement on "I hardly know her", which is what you've said in the past. So she's still succeeding in driving you crazy, eh? Way to go, Nic.'

'Steph, this is hardly helping.'

'Look.' She thought quickly, deciding to bluff his real feelings out into the open. 'There's another reason why I called. Oliver has a friend coming to town tomorrow morning and we thought it would be nice to introduce him to Nicolette.'

'Why?'

Stephanie smiled. Not only could she feel his tension increase, she could hear it in his voice. If only it were this easy with Oliver, but she was sure that if she pretended to be interested in another man he would merely shrug and wish her all the best. Then again, he *had* been jealous of Stephen earlier on. Hmm. Something for her to ponder. Right now, though, she needed to sort out her brother. 'Because she's a nice person, she's single and this guy sounds like her type.'

'I'm a nice person, I'm single and how on earth would you know what her type is?' he growled fiercely.

'I'm her friend. Girls talk.' Stephanie began to giggle and then he caught on.

'You're playing me.'

'So how did you feel, eh? Does the thought of Nicolette with any other man make you crazy? Personally, I think the answer is yes,' she went on before he could say a word.

'Well, if you want to talk about romance, Steph, let me give you a little quiz about Oliver.'

'Oh, gee. Is that the time? I have to go now, bro.' She laughed. 'See you later. Love you.' She hung up and stood, grabbing her bag. Not only did she not want to talk about Oliver, right now she didn't even want to think about him. She needed to focus on her job and put him right out of her mind.

'Easier said than done,' she mumbled as she walked out of her room.

Stephanie had been at work for just over three hours, with no sign of Oliver, when she was given the case of a seventeen-year-old girl who had a sewing needle through her finger. Her mother had opted to stay in the waiting room, saying she was 'no good in hospitals'.

'That's certainly interesting,' Stephanie said as she looked at Amy's finger. 'What were you sewing?' She turned away and checked the X-rays she'd sent Amy for on arrival.

'Denim. I've been under a lot of pressure lately because my assignment is already two weeks past deadline, and with all my other subjects, things just seem to pile up.'

'Carelessness?'

'I guess…' She shrugged. 'And I'm really tired. I didn't get to bed until three o'clock because I was trying to finish my history paper.' Amy winced a little as Stephanie touched the needle, which had gone right through the finger.

'I think a bit of local anaesthetic is in order. So what's your project for sewing class?'

'Industrial design—that's what the subject is.'

'Oh. Things have changed so much since I was at school. What are you making?'

'I'm doing a step-by-step booklet about how to turn your old denim jeans into a denim skirt.'

'Excellent.'

'My teacher doesn't think so. I'm the only girl in the class and he tends to patronise me. And even if my work is faultless, he finds something really small to mark me down on. It wouldn't matter so much except some of the boys, whose work is clearly below standard, get better marks for incomplete work!'

'You are under stress. What about registering a formal complaint?' Stephanie administered the local and set about getting the instruments she'd need.

'I've tried, but the principal is the teacher's brother-in-law and—'

'Your complaints are falling on deaf ears. That's not right.'

'I've only got this year to go and then I'm out of there. No more school for me.'

'No university?'

'My mum wants me to go but...' Amy shook her head. 'I want at least a year off just to relax.'

Stephanie smiled. 'Sounds good.' They continued chatting until the anaesthetic had done its job. 'All right. Let's get this needle out of your finger.'

'What happens then? Do I need to keep my hand bandaged?'

'I'm afraid so.'

Tears filled Amy's eyes. 'But I won't be able to finish.'

'I'll be giving you a doctor's certificate and if necessary speaking to the teacher in question myself. The pressure you kids get put under today...' Stephanie shook her head as she concentrated on her job. She heard the curtain around

Amy's bed slide back and glanced up briefly, surprised to see Oliver there.

'Hi,' she said, and returned her attention to her work. Oliver introduced himself to Amy and heard the teenager's tale of woe while Stephanie managed to extract the needle cleanly and without complication.

'You'll need to soak it daily so it can heal from the inside out,' Stephanie said as she bathed the finger before bandaging it. She went to give Amy a few extra bandages but realised the cubicle was not stocked properly. 'I'll be back in a moment,' she said, sliding the curtain open and heading out. She returned five minutes later with bandages and instructions for Amy, as well as a doctor's certificate and note for her teacher.

'If he has any problems with that, you call me and I'll speak to him personally. I know the experts say the pressure on students in their final year is to prepare them for the outside world—and in some ways they're right. You're always going to come across someone who doesn't give you a fair deal, whether they're a co-worker or your boss, but at your age the pressure shouldn't be so much that you end up completely frazzled.'

Amy nodded, tears welling in her eyes.

'You have bags under your eyes, you're exhausted and you need a good, uncomplicated sleep.'

'She's a regular flatterer,' Oliver said jokingly to Amy. 'But she's right. I know you're under pressure but try and get some rest.'

'Paracetamol will help with the pain.'

'OK.'

Stephanie walked Amy out to the waiting room and very briefly explained to Amy's mother what had happened. The other woman's face went pale so Stephanie cut things short. 'Here are the X-rays and the rest of the paperwork.' She handed them over. 'Good luck with the project, Amy, and when you've finished the booklet, please, drop a copy off so I can learn how to do it. It sounds like a terrific idea.'

'I'll do that. Thanks again. I've felt better just talking about things.'

'Make sure you see your GP in two weeks' time to have that finger checked,' she reminded her, before heading back to the nurses' station to write up the notes.

'All done?' Oliver asked over her shoulder, making her jump.

'Yes.' She turned and looked up at him. They were in the exact the same positions as his first night at the hospital—the night when she'd stood and kissed him on the cheek. It seemed so long ago instead of the couple of weeks it had been since she'd met him...and now she was in love with him! She supposed her life could never be called dull.

'Er...' He cleared his throat and she realised she'd been staring. 'So, can you come to my office when you have a spare ten minutes? I need to talk to you.'

Stephanie met his gaze, noticing how it had darkened with desire from her appraisal. 'I'm free now.'

'OK.' Unable to control the temptation to touch her, he reached for her hand and helped her to her feet. He reluctantly dropped it as they walked through the department and to his office. Once there, he closed the door and motioned for her to sit.

'So? What's up, boss?'

'Nothing bad. I just wanted to share some good news with you.'

She waited, watching as a small smile creased his lips.

'I've just put in an offer for a house.'

Stephanie's jaw dropped open in shock. Of all the things she'd expected Oliver to say, that hadn't been one of them. 'I thought you called me here because you wanted to discuss work,' she said after a moment, before standing. 'Is that it?'

'What do you mean, "Is that it?" I wanted to share my good news with you.'

'Great. Thanks. Hope you'll be happy.' She headed for the door but Oliver was out of his chair and around the desk like a shot.

'Stephanie?' He placed his hands on her shoulders, searching her expression for some clue to explain her behaviour. He thought she'd be pleased, that she'd be interested in his life. After all, she'd professed to love him. 'What's going on?'

'Nothing.' She stepped back and he dropped his hands.

'Don't lie to me. I can tell there's something wrong. Someone meeting you for the first time could see there was something wrong.'

'I just can't do this any more.'

'What? What can't you do?'

Stephanie shook her head, desperate to keep the threatening tears under control. 'Feel as though I'm some sort of consolation prize.'

'Who makes you feel like that?'

Stephanie stared at him, totally amazed. '*You* do. You ask me to help you at work—so I help you. You ask me to help you with your daughter—so I do. I'm not begrudging that, honestly, I'm not. I like helping people. It's why I became a doctor, but this…' She waved her hand between the two of them. 'I just can't do it any more.'

Oliver was completely taken aback.

'Everyone at work has accepted the changes and things are running smoothly. You've been able to open up to Kaz and the two of you are going to be fine. And now…now you've bought a house and so you no longer need the place you're staying in. That's great. It's wonderful. For *you*. But what about me, Oliver? What were your plans for me? A little interlude while you got yourself settled here? A bit of

fun?' Her voice choked on the word and the tears fell from
her eyelashes. She brushed them away impatiently.

'But it all backfired, didn't it?' Her tone was filled with
scorn and distaste—both emotions aimed at herself rather
than Oliver. 'You hadn't planned on me falling in love with
you. Ever since I told you, you've been reserved and distant
and you've made it quite clear that you wanted out of the
house.' She hiccuped, cross with herself for getting so emo-
tional, but she couldn't help it. A woman should be allowed
to cry when her heart was being broken.

'I've been a prize fool, haven't I? How ridiculous was it
that I fell in love with a man who never wanted the love
of any woman again? I guess that's just my annoying in-
experience rearing its ugly head.' She pulled a tissue from
her pocket and blew her nose. 'Well, I'm sorry, Oliver. I'm
sorry I'm not excited about your new house. I'm sorry I'm
not going to fall at your feet, doing your bidding any more,
and I'm sorry I ever thought myself in love with you.'

CHAPTER TEN

OLIVER let her go.

He stood there, totally stunned at her words and the pain he could not only see in her face but hear in her voice. Exactly how long he stood there he wasn't sure, staring at the closed door to his office as though it would hopefully bring her back.

It didn't.

'She needs time,' he mumbled as he finally sat back down in his chair. He picked up a piece of paper but threw it back on the desk a second later, shaking his head and rubbing his hand over his eyes. How had he let things get so out of hand?

Oliver sucked in a breath and exhaled slowly, trying to make sense of what had just happened. He'd never meant to hurt her. He cared about her. In such a short space of time she'd become more than a colleague, more than a friend…more than a girlfriend?

Was there any truth in what she'd said? Had he really behaved so badly? He'd been upfront about what he'd needed from her, especially regarding the staff and the changes here at the hospital. He hadn't asked her to lie or be deceptive, not that she was capable of either. Stephanie was an honest woman and he'd realised that from their earliest acquaintance.

The phone on his desk shrilled to life and he snatched it up, thankful for the distraction. 'Dr Bowan.'

'Oliver. It's Stephen.'

Oliver closed his eyes, trying to stifle a groan. How was

he supposed to stop thinking about Stephanie now? 'What can I do for you?'

'I'd like to talk about Steph.'

Oliver shook his head and opened his eyes, looking unseeingly at the work on his desk. 'Going to read me my rights?'

'Pardon?'

'You know, do the over-protective brother thing and bawl me out for treating your sister badly? If you are, then I have to say now is not a good time.'

Stephen was silent for a moment. 'Have you?'

'Treated her badly?' Oliver raked his free hand through his hair. 'Probably. I don't know. I'm rather confused at the moment. I take it from the fact you're calling me that you've *felt* her anguish and spoken to her.'

'She wouldn't talk. She just said she'd be around tonight to stay over. So I thought I'd get the scoop from you.'

'What? You're not going to tell her I'm all wrong for her? That I'm a divorced, single father who has more problems than her inexperienced heart can handle?'

'You seem to be under the impression that I want you and Steph to stop seeing each other.'

'Don't you?'

'You've told me you respect her and I believe you. Besides, since you arrived her emotions have been in a constant state of flux.'

'Really? Is that a good thing?'

'It's good for Steph. With the few relationships she's had, she's always been in control. She would call the shots and she would walk away without getting too badly hurt. In fact, with the majority of the men she's dated, she's stayed friends with most of them. What happened was that she never really put herself out there, put her heart on the line. With you, she has. She's in love with you.'

'I know.'

Silence again from Stephen. 'And do you love her?'

'It's a question I seem to be getting asked quite frequently of late.'

'Do you have the guts to answer it?'

'Do you?'

'She's told you about Nicolette and I,' Stephen stated, then chuckled humourlessly. 'Looks as though we're both in the same boat.'

'Stephanie's positive you'll end up together. She says Nicolette is perfect for you.'

'So she's told me.'

'She's not one to keep her cards close to her chest.'

'Steph? You'd be surprised, Oliver. She only shares the positive things.'

'Meaning?'

'She may have told you she loves you but she'll hide all the pain and heartbreak she's feeling right now. She'll lock herself up so tight even I'll have trouble penetrating her emotions.'

'She's supposed to come to Sydney with Kaz and me tomorrow.'

'She told me.'

'But you said she's staying at your house tonight.'

'Yes. She'll be there. She'll go to Sydney with you because she doesn't want to let Kaz down. She's one amazing woman, Oliver.'

'You don't need to convince me.'

'Obviously I do, otherwise you'd know whether or not you're in love with her.'

'Does this mean I have your approval?'

'You have the power to give her either the greatest joy she's ever felt or the greatest pain.'

'Very prophetic words.'

'Yes, and I've just realised they apply as much to me as

they do to you. Looks as though we both have a lot of thinking to do.'

'I appreciate your call, Stephen.' Oliver hung up and sat there, staring at the telephone, letting Stephen's words slowly sink in.

The next morning, Oliver dragged himself out of bed and went to have breakfast. He'd stayed up until two o'clock, hoping Stephanie might have changed her mind and come home. *Home?* The old saying about home being where the heart was flashed through his mind, and he groaned.

'Something wrong, dear?' Mrs Dixon asked as he sat down at the kitchen bench.

'When isn't something wrong, Mrs D.? Any coffee?'

'You look exhausted. I think this trip to Sydney will do you all the world of good. Clear away some cobwebs.'

'You're not coming?'

'Oh, no. The thought of having today and tomorrow all to myself, to sit and read a book uninterrupted, is too good to pass up. Besides, I don't want to get in the way.'

'Very tactful of you,' Oliver muttered as Kasey walked in, all bright-eyed and bushy-tailed. 'Good morning, Kaz.'

'Morning, Dad. Is Steph not up yet?'

Oliver looked from his daughter to Mrs Dixon and back again. Kasey was going to have a fit when she realised Stephanie wasn't here and, more to the point, that *he* was the reason Stephanie wasn't here. 'Well…'

'She called last night,' Mrs Dixon interrupted him, 'when you were in bed, Kasey. She spent the night at her brother's house. It seems she needed to discuss some things with him.'

'Oh.' Kasey frowned then looked at her father. 'Did you know about it?'

'It was mentioned to me.' Oliver and Mrs Dixon shared another look.

'OK,' Kasey demanded. 'What's going on? You two are acting really strange.' When neither adult spoke, she continued, 'Look, I may only be eight years old but I'm not stupid. I can tell when there's something wrong. Dad, were you a jerk to Steph?'

'What?'

'Is that why she stayed at her brother's?'

'Uh...'

'Kasey, show a little respect for your father.'

'No. She's right, Mrs Dixon, and she has every right to question me. Stephanie and I had a...discussion yesterday and, yes, she was mad at me. But rest assured, I intend to put things right because even being in this house without her doesn't seem right.'

He'd felt guilty about making her leave. She felt hurt and humiliated and it was all because of him. Well, he'd always been a man who took responsibility for his actions and this was no exception.

'What do you mean?' Kasey asked sceptically.

A smile touched Oliver's lips as he felt his mood begin to lift. 'I have a plan. Want to help me?'

'Will it make Stephanie happy?'

'I hope it will make *all* of us happy.'

Kasey jumped up and down and clapped her hands. 'Goody.'

Stephanie pulled up outside the house just before ten. Oliver hadn't called Stephen's house to hurry her up, so she presumed he was waiting for her. Either that or he'd just gone and left her behind.

She closed her eyes as she switched off the engine, not wanting to think about it. If he wasn't inside, if he had left, that would be the final nail in their relationship. The unmistakable sign that it was over. She opened her sore eyes and took a deep breath, deciding she couldn't put off the inevitable any longer.

No sooner had she taken a few steps towards the house than Kasey came hurtling outside, almost throwing herself into Stephanie's arms.

'You're here.'

Stephanie hugged the girl back, fresh tears filling her eyes as the relief that they were still there swamped her.

'Why are you crying?' Kasey asked when she pulled back. She slipped her hand into Stephanie's and tugged her inside. 'Are you all right?'

Stephanie sniffed with happiness. 'I'm good. Just a little fragile.'

'Yeah. Dad told me he was a jerk to you yesterday.'

Stephanie raised her eyebrows at this information and the hope inside her grew a little more.

'Come on, Dad said we're leaving in half an hour. I'm not sure what to wear. What do you wear to go shopping?'

'Comfortable shoes,' Stephanie replied automatically, and both of them giggled as they reached the house.

'Is that all? Just comfortable shoes?' Oliver was standing by the door, dressed in denim jeans and a royal blue polo shirt, which highlighted the magnificent colour of his eyes. He looked gorgeous and undeniably sexy. The small smile that touched his lips was one she'd been aching all night long to see. The scent of him teased her and her eyelids fluttered closed for a moment before she tried desperately to pull herself together. Why was it that thirty seconds in his presence turned her to mush? His eyebrows were raised in question and she realised he was waiting for an answer.

'Well, perhaps some clothes, but definitely comfortable ones.' She forced her gaze away from his. 'Although, if you go shopping in *uncomfortable* clothes, it means you definitely have to buy new ones and wear them immediately.'

Kasey laughed. 'Yes, yes. Let's do that.'

Oliver groaned. 'This trip is going to be more expensive than I thought.'

'Daddy!' Kasey groaned, and glared at him as though he was giving away some secret.

'What? I was just making a comment. Come on, you two. Get packed because we're out of here in thirty minutes and no later.'

Kasey tugged Stephanie into her room. 'Do you have a bag? We need a bag. I'm already packed. In fact, I was packed last night. I did it by myself but then, I'm kind of used to it. But it was good, packing clothes that weren't school uniform.' She squealed excitedly. 'I can't believe I don't need to go back to that school. That I'm going to stay with my dad for ever.'

Stephanie laughed at Kasey's animation. 'I'm really happy for you.'

'Come *on*, Steph. Will you pack already?'

'Sorry.' Stephanie did as she was told and it wasn't until they were ready to get into the car that she realised she hadn't booked accommodation in Sydney. Before she could voice her thoughts, another problem arose. Mrs Dixon was hugging both Kasey and Oliver goodbye! 'You're not coming, Mrs D.?'

'Oh, no, dear. I've done enough travelling in the last few weeks to last me quite a while. You all go and have a good time, and I'll look after the house.'

There was nothing Stephanie could do because Oliver had climbed behind the wheel of his hire car and was starting the engine.

'Come on, Steph. Put your seat belt on,' Kasey demanded.

Feeling highly self-conscious, she climbed in, shut the door and buckled up. She wasn't sure whether or not to say something to Oliver. If he'd told her Mrs Dixon wasn't coming, she wouldn't have come… And then it hit her. Oliver *wanted* her to come.

She glanced surreptitiously at him, wondering if she dared let her hope increase yet again. He had his sunglasses on and was concentrating on the road as he reversed, tooting the horn and waving goodbye to Mrs D.

'So, Kaz. You get first pick of the music. Which CDs did you pack?'

Kasey named her favourite artist—the one whose picture Stephanie had printed out for her. 'He's *s-o-o* nice.'

'Excellent,' Stephanie said, and took the CD Kasey passed over. She inserted it and soon they were both singing along to the songs while Oliver listened, a bemused smile on his face.

'Both of you have such sweet voices,' he said.

Stephanie laughed, enjoying herself. 'I know Kaz's voice is unbelievable, but I think even "sweet" is going a little too far in my case. I'm not completely tone deaf but close to it.'

The time seemed to pass more quickly than usual and before Stephanie knew it they were down from the mountains, heading for the motorway to Sydney's centre. It was then she remembered about the accommodation.

'Uh…where are you two staying?'

'The same place as you.' Oliver glanced over, smiling at her. He named the hotel and her eyebrows rose.

'Pretty expensive.'

'This is Sydney. Everywhere is expensive. This weekend is a special occasion.' He glanced in the rear-view mirror. 'Isn't that right, Kaz?'

'Yep. I'm gonna tell that lawyer that I'm staying with my dad.'

Oliver winked at his daughter and she winked right back. Stephanie felt as though she'd just missed something, but as some idiot driver pulled out from nowhere, causing

Oliver to swerve and slam on the brakes, she didn't say anything.

'You both all right? I'd forgotten what it's like, driving in Sydney. I think I'd better concentrate more,' he muttered, shaking his head.

Stephanie switched off the music so Oliver could concentrate, and they made it to the hotel without further mishap. 'I'd forgotten how stressful Sydney traffic is.' He handed the keys to the valet after they'd taken out their overnight bags. 'Let's get checked in.'

'What time's your appointment with the solicitor?'

'He's a friend from school so he told me to give him a call once we were settled.'

'Oh. You mean the snooty boarding school you went to?'

Oliver smiled at her and she felt her heart flutter with happiness. 'One and the same. You're welcome to come with us.'

'*Dad!*' Kasey glowered but Oliver waved her concerns away.

Stephanie once more looked from one to the other. 'That's all right. I was hoping to catch up with a few friends from med school. They're at Royal North Shore so I'll spend time there while you're busy.'

'And then we're going shopping, right?'

Stephanie laughed. 'Right, and then more shopping tomorrow.'

'Yee-ha.'

'Looks as though I'll have time to myself as well. After all…' he glanced down at his jeans '…I'm still not wearing a dress.'

Kasey giggled. 'So you can't come shopping. It's just me and Steph.'

'Steph and I,' both adults corrected her, then laughed.

Once Oliver had checked them in, they were shown to

two adjoining rooms. 'You two can sleep in one and I get the other all to myself,' Oliver teased.

'Unfair.' Kasey pouted. 'I think you and Steph should share and *I* get one to myself.'

Oliver met Stephanie's gaze and she could instantly feel her face becoming flushed. Nothing had been sorted out. From all the things she'd said to him yesterday afternoon, nothing had been sorted. They'd just called some weird truce—a truce she didn't know the rules to—and she could feel herself beginning to panic deep inside.

Her mouth went dry and she swallowed, feeling swamped with shyness. She saw the flash of desire in his eyes and knew her own reciprocated the awareness, even though she wasn't quite sure where she stood. She loved him, he wanted to date her. That's where they'd left things. Was this weekend supposed to show her it would be enough…at least until Oliver decided he didn't want her any more?

'I think we'll keep things the way they are,' Oliver told his daughter, and Stephanie wondered whether the words were aimed at her and the status of their relationship.

Thankfully, she seemed to find her brain again and looked away, putting her bag onto the end of one of the beds.

'Just think, we can have girl talk all night long. We can paint our toenails and put curlers in our hair.' She paused as she spoke and Kasey giggled. 'Hmm. Perhaps we'll just put the curlers in your hair.'

'Might be a bit hard in yours,' Oliver agreed.

'Which reminds me, I need to make some phone calls.'

'Who are you calling?' Oliver asked.

'Ah, now, that's important girl stuff and as you've already pointed out, Dr Bowan, you're not wearing a dress so…out.' She pointed to the connecting door.

'Unfair,' he grumbled, but left them alone.

'Who *are* you calling?' Kasey said once he'd left.

'My hairdresser. It's time to decide on a new colour.'

Stephanie was able to catch up with her friends while Oliver and Kasey went to see his solicitor. As she caught a taxi back to the hotel, late in the afternoon, she hoped everything had gone well for father and daughter. It was a strange situation and she wondered whether it bothered Oliver that his ex-wife might one day marry his brother? Kasey's uncle would become her stepfather but, hopefully, she wouldn't have to see them that often.

Back at the hotel, she found Kasey impatiently waiting for her. 'We finished ages ago.'

'Don't exaggerate, Kaz.' Oliver laughed and turned to face Stephanie. 'We've only been back for half an hour—if that. Have fun visiting your friends?'

'Yes. It's always good to see them.' Although this time she'd felt rather disjointed. It was as though her friends were from a different part of her life—her life before Oliver. Had she really changed that much in such a short time?

'Are we going shopping or what?' Kasey demanded. Stephanie checked her watch.

'The shops are open for about another half an hour so we'd better hustle. Then we can finish tomorrow.'

They went to a few shops closest to them and Stephanie bought Kasey a bracelet with KAZ on it. 'Something to remember me by.'

'Are you going somewhere?'

Stephanie shrugged. 'Things may not always be as they are now.'

'You mean between you and my dad? No. I guess they won't.' Kasey's smile was broad, her eyes sparkling. It puzzled Stephanie.

'We'd better get back in time for dinner.'

Oliver was waiting downstairs for them in the hotel restaurant and Stephanie was thankful they weren't going out
again. She was exhausted. Too much thinking, trying to
decipher expressions or little snippets of information. She
was thankful when Oliver declared it time for bed.

'I was just going to excuse myself.'

'I'm not surprised. That's about the tenth time you've
yawned in the last few minutes.'

Stephanie smiled as they rode the lift up, Kasey snuggled
in her father's arms. 'Sorry. I didn't mean you were boring
company.'

'I understand.' He stopped outside their door and waited
for her to open it.

'Do you?'

He placed Kasey on the bed and took off the girl's shoes
before pulling the covers around her. Then he straightened
and walked over to Stephanie.

'I understand completely,' he declared firmly, and she
knew they were talking about something completely different. They stood, gazing into each other's eyes, the world
around them disappearing. He brushed his fingers over her
cheek, his thumb gently caressing her lips which parted
immediately, letting him know they were desperate for his
touch.

'Steph,' he sighed, his eyes darkening with desire, but
he made no move to kiss her. He wanted nothing more than
to be with her but knew he had to take it slowly, especially
if he wanted his plan to come to fruition. With superhuman
effort he dropped his hand and took two steps towards his
door. 'Get some sleep.' His voice was deep and husky with
repressed emotion. 'I've booked us in for breakfast at nine
so sleep in if Kaz lets you.'

In the next breath he was gone and Stephanie was left
to have another fitful sleep, wet tears falling silently onto
her pillow. In the morning she felt even more miserable

than she had the previous day. It was then she realised that the emotions she was experiencing weren't just her own. 'Not now, Stephen,' she muttered as she showered. Thankfully, Kasey had slept right through until just after eight o'clock and had then watched television while Stephanie had eventually given up all pretence of sleep and decided to get the day started.

They were halfway through breakfast when she suddenly felt a huge weight lift from her shoulders. 'Excuse me,' she said, pulling her cellphone from her pocket as she stood. 'I just need to check on Stephen.'

Oliver glanced up. 'Everything all right?'

'Feels that way to me.' She smiled brightly at him, unable to believe how happy she felt. 'Back in a minute.'

Oliver watched her walk away before going over the plan with Kasey. He glanced again in the direction Stephanie had gone, wondering about her brother. Had Stephen found the answers to his own questions?

All was revealed when Stephanie eventually came back, brushing tears away. 'What's wrong?' Oliver was out of his chair, his hands on her shoulders as he gazed down into her face. Then he realised she didn't look upset…she looked happy.

'Nothing's wrong. Everything's just perfect.'

'What's going on?' Kasey demanded.

'Stephen and Nicolette just got engaged.'

'Just then?' Oliver smiled, happy for her and for her brother.

'Yes. They let me listen to the proposal and be involved and everything, and it was so great and now I just want to see them.'

'But what about shopping?' Kasey wailed.

Stephanie laughed. 'We are not postponing shopping. I have to find the perfect outfit for my brother's wedding.'

'Do you think I'll be invited?'

'I'm certain of it. So, if you've finished eating, let's get this shopping day organised.' She turned to face Oliver. 'No dress?'

'No. I don't have the legs for it.'

She laughed again, amazed at how happy she felt after being so miserable for the last few days. 'Perhaps we should get you a kilt. Surely, with the surname of Bowan, you have some Scottish ancestors somewhere.'

'Now, there's a thought. If I wear a kilt, can I join in with the girl stuff?'

'No!' Kasey wailed, and grabbed Stephanie's hand. 'Let's go, Steph. Bye, Dad.'

Stephanie shrugged as she snatched up her bag.

'I'll call you with details about lunch.'

'OK,' she agreed, before Kasey dragged her from the restaurant. The two of them shopped until they dropped and Stephanie was surprised how much fun shopping with an eight-year-old could be. 'You definitely have a shoe fetish,' she told Kasey. 'You've already bought two new pairs. Do you really need these boots?'

'But they're so good. They're purple.'

'Yes. I wish they had them in my size. What's the price?' They checked the ticket and when they found they were half-price, Stephanie didn't even hesitate in carrying them to the counter and paying for them. 'Shopping is great but getting a bargain is even greater.'

'I want to wear them.'

'Yes. They match your new outfit perfectly.'

'I love that new dress. The burgundy colour goes great with your new hair colour.'

Stephanie laughed. 'I can't believe you talked me into wearing it. It's a bit flash just to go shopping in.'

'But this is a special weekend, remember?' Kasey smiled. 'I can't believe we have the same hair colour. It was so cool, watching you get it done. I like it.'

'Does that mean you like your colour now?'

She thought about it for a moment. 'You know, I think I do. And mine's *natural*.'

Stephanie laughed as Kasey changed her shoes, the purple patent-leather boots topping off her outfit. 'We look fit for lunch with the Queen.'

'Who's the Queen?' Kasey asked as the sales assistant boxed up her old shoes and handed them over.

'Oh, Kaz. You've been living in America too long.'

'Duh. Only all my life...until now.'

Stephanie's phone rang. 'That'll be your dad.'

'Having fun?' he asked.

'Definitely.'

'Almost done?'

Stephanie checked her watch, surprised to find it was half past one. 'I think we're definitely in need of sustenance.'

'Good. Where are you?' She gave him the name of the store. 'Be outside the main entrance in five minutes.'

'OK.' She disconnected the call and was stunned when five minutes later a limousine pulled into the kerb and Oliver got out. 'Oliver!' She looked him up and down. 'You look...' She shook her head, unable to find the words to describe how incredible he looked in a tux.

'I was just thinking the same thing about you. I really like the hair.'

She smiled shyly under his gaze.

'What do you think of my new outfit, Daddy?'

Oliver somehow managed to tear his gaze from Stephanie to look at his daughter. 'You look so grown-up. You're very beautiful, Kaz.' Then he frowned. 'Did you get your ears pierced?'

'No way. They're clip-ons. Steph said I should wait till I'm a bit older.'

He looked back at Stephanie. 'She's a wise woman.' He winked conspiratorially at Kasey. 'And she should know, she has so many earrings. Now, shall we go to lunch?' The chauffeur came and relieved them of their many shopping bags before Oliver helped Kasey into the car. Then he turned to Stephanie, his gaze washing over hers once more. *'Mademoiselle?'* He offered his hand.

'Monsieur.' When she placed her hand in his, she had the strange sensation she'd just come home. It was odd. 'So where are we going, or is it a surprise?'

'Sydney Tower.'

'To the revolving restaurant?'

'Yes. Problem?'

She pretended to consider him thoughtfully. 'I'm concerned you can't handle it. From what I've heard, you get sick on dizzy rides.'

Oliver pointed his finger at Kasey. 'Someone told you about Disneyland.' Kasey merely giggled. 'Thankfully, the restaurant doesn't go around *that* fast.'

When they arrived, and after going through the metal detectors, they were whisked up in the high-speed lift, their ears popping. At the gallery level, they exited and went through to the reception lounge, where they were greeted by the restaurant's hostess.

'Welcome, Dr Brooks, Ms Bowan and Dr Bowan,' the hostess said. 'This way.'

Stephanie frowned. 'How did she know my name?' It wasn't until they were shown to their table that Stephanie realised they were the only ones in the restaurant.

'Surprise!' Kasey said, clapping her hands excitedly. 'Now you see why you *had* to wear your new dress? So we could all be in our bestest clothes for lunch.'

Stephanie's gaze met Oliver's. 'I don't understand. Is this because you have custody of Kaz?'

'Partly. Please, have a seat.' He glanced at Kasey. 'Now or later?'

'Now. Now. Do it now.' The eight-year-old was bubbling with excitement.

'Yes. I can't wait either.' He motioned for the hostess and she wheeled over a trolley. On the trolley were two bunches of Australian wildflowers and two tiny boxes… jewellery boxes. Oliver handed one box to Kasey and took the other one for himself. 'You first, honey.'

'OK.' Kasey came around and gave Stephanie a hug.

'No,' Oliver said. 'Wait a second.' He pulled his cellphone from his pocket. 'We need to call Stephen.'

'Good idea.' Kasey gave Stephanie another hug, climbing onto her lap. 'Isn't this exciting?'

'I…' Stephanie swallowed, unsure what was going on, but knew, whatever it was, it was something vitally important to each and every one of them. 'Yes.'

'Stephen,' Oliver said into his phone, and Stephanie wondered how he'd got Stephen's number before she remembered Oliver had access to it at the hospital. 'It's Oliver. I hear congratulations are in order.'

'Yes. Is Steph all right?'

'I think so. Her hair is now a beautiful reddish-orange and it completely suits her, as does the beautiful dress she's wearing.'

'Steph's in a dress? Is that why she's apprehensive, or is there another reason?'

'There's definitely another reason and Kaz and I would like you to witness it… well, listen to it.' He shook his head. 'We'll just get on with it.' He placed the phone on the table and nodded to Kasey.

'OK.' Kasey handed Stephanie the box. 'Open it.'

Stephanie did as she was told and gasped when she saw the most gorgeous pair of emerald earrings nestled there.

'I love you, Steph. You're so much fun and you make me and my dad happy. Please, be my stepmom?'

Stephanie didn't even make an effort to stop the tears that flowed down her cheeks.

'You have to, you know, because we have the same hair colour.'

Both Stephanie and Oliver chuckled, their gazes blending.

'Now it's your turn, Dad.'

Oliver nodded and went down on one knee. 'Stephanie, what Kaz said is so true. You make us both so happy and it's because you love with such a generous spirit. In a very short time you've made me understand and feel wholeheartedly what true love is all about. I not only want to apologise for being so slow to realise it but I want to remedy the situation right now.' He opened the box and there was the most perfect emerald ring with a circlet of diamonds twinkling around it. 'I love you, Stephanie. Please, accept me as your husband.'

Stephanie looked at him through blurry eyes and sniffed again. 'Dad. We forgot tissues,' Kasey whispered, but a moment later a box appeared and Stephanie was able to wipe her eyes and blow her nose.

'Are you thinking about it? If you are, I don't blame you.' Oliver gazed at her with love and a hint of uncertainty. 'I was such a jerk not to realise sooner just how I felt about you.'

Stephanie reached out and placed a finger over his lips, silencing him. 'How could you even think I'd refuse? I love you, Oliver.'

He stood and, breaking the drought, pressed his mouth to hers. For both of them, it was as though they had truly come home.

'Hey. You're squashing me.'

Oliver and Stephanie laughed as they broke apart, both of them kissing Kasey—one on each side.

'I love you, too,' Stephanie said. 'So much. And I'd be honoured to be your stepmum.'

'It's *mom*.'

They all laughed and then Stephanie remembered the phone on the table. She picked it up. 'Hi, bro.'

'Hey, yourself. Nice going.'

'You, too. How's Nic?'

'Doubly excited now.'

Stephanie laughed. 'I'm glad you were listening.'

'Tell Oliver I appreciate it. He's perfect for you.'

Stephanie smiled at the man of her dreams, who was sliding the emerald ring onto her finger. 'You've got that right. I'm going to go now. Love you.' She rang off. She admired the ring on her finger. 'It's so perfect.'

'It had to be green because, no matter what colour your hair is, the emerald will remind us of what colour it was when we met.'

'Put the earrings in,' Kasey suggested, and Stephanie complied.

'I've asked the estate agent to hold off putting the offer in until you've had a good look over the house. Kaz likes it and so do I but you need to like it, too. If you don't we'll find one we can all grow old together in.'

Stephanie inserted the earrings and, after admiring them, Kasey walked off to ask about lunch, declaring herself very hungry.

'I'm so sorry, Steph,' Oliver said, sitting down and dragging her onto his lap, his arms securely around her. 'I was scared to take a chance. Things went so wrong with Nadele that I wasn't sure I could put my heart on the line again. You've taught me how to trust, how to give and how to love. For years I've been trying to get home. The only problem was, I had no idea where home was. Now...' He pressed his lips to hers. 'Now...I'm finally there and it' perfect. You are perfect for me and I have to warn you, I can't get enough of you.'

Their lips met and in the kisses they shared there were no unanswered questions, no wondering, no unknown factors. There was truth, respect and a powerfully consuming love.

'Are you two still mooching?' Kasey demanded, as she returned and sat down. 'Well, you can keep on going but I was sick of waiting for lunch so I've ordered—for all of us.'

Grinning widely, she looked over her shoulder. The hostess was wheeling out another trolley, this one filled with desserts.

'Lunch according to an eight-year-old.' Oliver shook his head and smiled.

'Hey. This is also lunch according to a thirty-five-year-old,' Stephanie told him.

'Women!' Oliver rolled his eyes. 'Should I start praying for a son now?'

Stephanie smiled and winked at Kasey. 'It couldn't hurt. Then again, it may be twins.'

Oliver groaned. 'Heaven help me!'

MILLS & BOON®

Live the emotion

Her Latin Lover's Revenge

When only seduction will settle the score!

In November 2005, By Request brings back three favourite romances by our bestselling Mills & Boon authors:

Don Joaquin's Revenge by Lynne Graham
A Sicilian Seduction by Michelle Reid
Lazaro's Revenge by Jane Porter

Don't miss these passionate stories!

On sale 4th November 2005

*Available at most branches of WHSmith, Tesco, ASDA,
Borders, Eason, Sainsbury's and most bookshops*

Visit www.millsandboon.co.uk

Look forward to all these
★ ★ wonderful books this ★
Christmas ★

BETTY
NEELS
MARGARET WAY
JESSICA STEELE
All I want for
Christmas

MILLS & BOON

When baby's delivered just in time for Christmas!

Precious Gifts

Marion Lennox · Josie Metcalfe
Kate Hardy

Together for
Christmas

Lynnette Kent & Sherryl Woods

Christmas

Jasmine Cresswell · Kate Hoffmann
Tara Taylor Quinn

MILLS & BOON

The
CHRISTMAS
VISIT

Margaret Moore
Gail Ranstrom
Terri Brisbin

SILHOUETTE
**SNOWY
NIGHTS**

HEATHER GRAHAM · LINDSAY McKENNA
MARILYN PAPPANO · ANNETTE BROADRICK

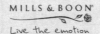

MILLS & BOON®

Live the emotion

Medical
romance™

A CHILD TO CALL HER OWN by *Gill Sanderson*

Dr Tom Ramsey is enchanted by the clinic's new midwife – she rekindles emotions Tom thought he'd never feel again. But midwife Maria Wyatt is haunted by memories – memories that come flooding back when she meets Tom's adorable son James…

DELL OWEN MATERNITY: Midwives, doctors, babies – at the heart of a Liverpool hospital

COMING HOME FOR CHRISTMAS
by *Meredith Webber*

A&E specialist Nash McLaren has come home for Christmas, and is surprised to hear GP Ella Marsden is back. He thought no one in the town would trust a Marsden again. But, working with Ella, Nash starts to remember how good it feels to be with her…

EMERGENCY AT PELICAN BEACH
by *Emily Forbes*

Dr Tom Edwards has come to Pelican Beach to escape city life – meeting Dr Lexi Patterson after five years wasn't part of his plan! But, working together, they save lives, share memories and become close. The career-driven Lexi of the past has changed – she can't let Tom go again…

Don't miss out!
On sale 4th November 2005

researching the cure

The facts you need to know:

- **One woman in nine** in the United Kingdom will develop breast cancer during her lifetime.

- Each year **40,700** women are newly diagnosed with breast cancer and around **12,800** women will die from the disease. However, survival rates are improving, with on average 77 per cent of women still alive five years later.

- **Men can also suffer from breast cancer**, although currently they make up less than one per cent of all new cases of the disease.

Britain has one of the highest breast cancer death rates in the world. Breast Cancer Campaign wants to understand why and do something about it. Statistics cannot begin to describe the impact that breast cancer has on the lives of those women who are affected by it and on their families and friends.

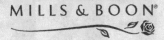

4 FREE

BOOKS AND A SURPRISE GIFT!

We would like to take this opportunity to thank you for reading this Mills & Boon® book by offering you the chance to take FOUR more specially selected titles from the Medical Romance™ series absolutely FREE! We're also making this offer to introduce you to the benefits of the Reader Service™—

- ★ FREE home delivery
- ★ FREE gifts and competitions
- ★ FREE monthly Newsletter
- ★ Exclusive Reader Service offers
- ★ Books available before they're in the shops

Accepting these FREE books and gift places you under no obligation to buy, you may cancel at any time, even after receiving your free shipment. Simply complete your details below and return the entire page to the address below. You don't even need a stamp!

YES! Please send me 4 free Medical Romance books and a surprise gift. I understand that unless you hear from me, I will receive 6 superb new titles every month for just £2.75 each, postage and packing free. I am under no obligation to purchase any books and may cancel my subscription at any time. The free books and gift will be mine to keep in any case.

M5ZED

Ms/Mrs/Miss/Mr .... Initials ....
                                                        BLOCK CAPITALS PLEASE
Surname ....
Address ....
....
.... Postcode ....

Send this whole page to:
UK: FREEPOST CN81, Croydon, CR9 3WZ

Offer valid in UK only and is not available to current Reader service subscribers to this series. Overseas and Eire please write for details. We reserve the right to refuse an application and applicants must be aged 18 years or over. Only one application per household. Terms and prices subject to change without notice. Offer expires 31st January 2006. As a result of this application, you may receive offers from Harlequin Mills & Boon and other carefully selected companies. If you would prefer not to share in this opportunity please write to The Data Manager, PO Box 676, Richmond, TW9 1WU.

Mills & Boon® is a registered trademark owned by Harlequin Mills & Boon Limited.
Medical Romance™ is being used as a trademark. The Reader Service™ is being used as a trademark.